The *Yankee* Billionaire's Bride

USA Today Bestselling Author

ROZ LEE

The Yankee Billionaire's Bride

ROZ LEE

DEDICATION

To the wonderful readers who
encourage me daily to keep writing.

ACKNOWLEDGMENTS

The actual writing of a book is a solitary task, but before a single reader sees the finished product, many hands and minds have touched it.

Many thanks to my fellow writers who listened to me complain as I worked through the issues with this story. A very special thanks to Diane Nelson who read an earlier version and whose comments led me to scrap the project and begin again.

I'd be remiss if I didn't thank my editor, Laura Garland at Wizards in Publishing for her keen eye and knowledge of grammar.

PART ONE

"If you love someone, set them free.
If they come back, they're yours; if they
don't, they never were."
Richard Bach

CHAPTER ONE

Roseanne Meadows stood on the busy Las Vegas sidewalk, watching the limo disappear with the newlyweds inside. Beside her, she could feel Scott Ramsey's gaze boring into her. He knew something was going on in her brain, but, to his credit, he'd said nothing during the wedding. If she knew anything about the man, it was that he wouldn't do anything to ruin his best friend's wedding. Just as she would have cut off her right arm rather than do anything to upset *her* best friend's wedding.

But Becky and Ford were married now, and all bets were off.

"What's wrong, Roseanne? And don't

tell me it's nothing because I know you better than that." He should. They'd been sleeping together for months. She'd let him get closer to her, emotionally and physically than anyone else—ever.

"Can we go home now? I think I've had enough of Vegas." Truth. She was finished. Done. Over it. But not over him. Not by a long shot. Maybe she never would be. That hurt more than anything else—knowing he didn't give two hoots about her when every cell in her body ached for him not to be the person she suspected him of being.

"You want to go home tonight? Don't you have a spa date with Becky tomorrow?"

She gave the man the evil eye. That date had been planned before Becky and Ford had decided on their hasty Vegas wedding chapel nuptials. "Seriously? Becky just got married. Do you really think she's going to want to hang out with me tomorrow?"

"Is that it? Are you worried that you've lost your best friend?"

She'd certainly lost something, but not

Becky. Married or not, her childhood friend would never desert her. Roseanne shook her head. "No. I didn't want to say anything to Becks, but I think I might be coming down with something."

"You're sick? Geez, why didn't you say so?" When he wrapped his arm around her waist, pulling her close, it was all she could do not to flinch. Twenty-four hours ago, she would have welcomed his embrace, but that was before. Now, everything he said or did felt false. "Do you need to see a doctor? I'm sure the hotel has one on call."

"I'd rather just go home, if you don't mind?" Home, where she could put this latest failure behind her. Or, at least bury herself in work and pretend Scott Ramsey hadn't ripped her heart out with his bare hands.

"Not at all. Our business here is done." He waved his arm, and the limo that had been waiting for them inched up to the curb. He handed her inside then joined her. After giving instructions to the driver, he made a phone call. "All set. The plane will be ready to go when we get there."

Must be nice. Had it only been a couple of days ago that they'd flown from Dallas to Las Vegas in Scott's private jet to help Ford and Becky at the sex toy trade show? It seemed like years had gone by, or maybe she was just feeling older. And wiser. Scott put his cell phone away and reached for her hand. Roseanne's stomach clenched at the contact, and a groan passed her lips.

"Are you all right? Can I get you anything? We can stop at a pharmacy if you want."

His voice held genuine concern, and, for the millionth time since his sister had cornered her at the convention center and given her an earful, she wondered if she was making the right decision to end her months-long relationship with the Yankee billionaire. Maybe Veronica was wrong. Maybe he just hadn't gotten around to asking her to attend his parents' anniversary party in New York next week. According to his sister, Scott had promised to attend.

In the face of his solicitude tonight, she could give him a few more days. If he didn't ask her to go with him, then she would know everything his sister had said was true. She was nothing more than a distraction for him while he attended to business in Butte Plains. As soon as he could, he'd hand the reins over to a manager and go back home to his high-society parties and glamorous women.

"No. I just think I need to rest. You have to admit, the last few days have been hectic."

"I thought we'd be here for moral support. I had no idea we'd get roped into manning the booth for hours each day."

"I don't think Ford and Becky anticipated how popular their booth would be. I'm sure they thought the interns they'd brought along would be able to handle the flow."

"Agreed. But I'll have a word with Ford if you're ill because of it."

As far as she knew, broken hearts weren't contagious or caused by spending a few hours standing on a concrete floor. "Don't. Please? I'm sure I'll be okay in a few days. I just need to rest." According to Veronica, Scott needed to be in New York by Friday night, which meant if he was going to ask her to go along, he would have to do it in the next few days. Heck, he hadn't even mentioned that *he* had a trip planned, which led her to believe he didn't want her to know about the party. Which meant everything his sister had said was true. Her stomach clenched again. This time, she barely managed to hold in the accompanying groan.

The limo crept along in the heavy traffic crowding the strip. Scott continued to hold her hand, and, rather than argue with him, she let it stay. This was all so stupid. She should just come right out and ask him about the party, but, deep down inside, she needed him to bring the subject up first. If he left for New York without telling her about the family event, she'd know the feelings she had for him weren't returned. They'd been sleeping together for several months. Not exactly living as a couple, but still, their relationship was intimate, and exclusive. Or so she thought.

That was the other bombshell

Veronica Ramsey had dropped on her. Scott had a girlfriend, or, to hear her tell it, a fiancé in all but the formal sense of the word. Solange. No last name. None needed. Everyone in the world knew the supermodel with the smile as bright as her name. According to his sister, Scott's family loved Solange and expected the couple to make it official as soon as Scott wrapped up his business in Texas.

At last, they made it to the hotel, packed up their things in the shared suite, and were on their way to the airport and the waiting Gulfstream aircraft.

As soon as they were wheels up, Roseanne disappeared to the bedroom in the rear of the cabin. No invitation to join her was given, and nothing about her demeanor or posture indicated he'd be welcome, so Scott remained in his seat, a drink in hand, and contemplated where their minivacation had gone wrong.

The woman who had occupied the seat next to him on the flight from Dallas to Las Vegas a few days ago was not the same one accompanying him home tonight. He would allow her some leeway for being ill, but that couldn't account for the deep chasm he sensed opening up between them. He was so out of his league with this woman. She was unlike any he'd ever dated. That alone had him wondering what the hell he was doing. None of the others had even come close to making him feel the way this one did—like he would never get enough of her and *afraid* he'd never get enough of her at the same time.

Fuck. I'm so screwed.

He'd known about his parents' anniversary party for months and gone back and forth in his mind whether he should invite Roseanne to accompany him to the milestone event. In Vegas, his sister had brought up the subject, asking to share the limo ride out to Long Island with him on the big day. He'd agreed, mentioning he might be bringing someone. That's when she'd reminded him of the time he'd made the mistake of taking a date to another such family gathering a few years ago. Before the last good-bye had been said, his mother had been contemplating which set of his grandmother's china she should give them as a wedding gift. He should have expected as much. The woman he'd taken had been just the kind of person his parents expected him to marry—born to wealth, well-educated, and runway model beautiful.

She'd been nothing but arm candy to him. It had taken him months to convince his mother one date didn't equal a marriage proposal.

He couldn't imagine what she would do if he showed up with Roseanne on his arm. She wasn't anything his parents wanted for him. June and Gerald Ramsey would never be impolite to a guest in their house, but there was a big difference between rude and welcoming. He couldn't bear the thought of Roseanne feeling out of place. As genuine and wholesome as homespun cloth, she was ten times better than most of the people who would be at the party, and far above the rest in every way that counted. Which led him to his other fear. His mother was so focused on her kids—

particularly him—settling down and producing babies for her to spoil, she might jump to the wrong conclusion and start talking about china patterns again. Lord help him if that happened. No matter what, he wouldn't be railroaded into marrying. One of these days, he'd take the plunge, but not before he was good and ready.

Then there was the very real possibility his parents would inform her about what a screw-up he was. No one could say the word entrepreneur quite the way his father could. For Christ's sake, you'd think Scott had become a criminal or something. They were better now than they were when he was a teenager and talked of going to MIT to become an engineer, but not by much. He could count on one hand the number of kids he'd grown up with who had gone on to finish college. As far as he knew, he was the only one to actually use the degree he'd earned. And *gasp*, made money! He'd never understood how that made him the screw-up in the family. You'd think his family was fucking royalty or something—too good to get their hands dirty.

Either way it turned out, he'd be screwed. Which was why he hadn't mentioned the party to Roseanne yet, and most likely wouldn't mention it. This was plainly one of those situations where what she didn't know wouldn't hurt her.

CHAPTER TWO

"How're you doing?" Kay Rogers appeared at the door to Roseanne's room. "I brought you something to help settle your stomach." She set a tray laden with tea and crackers on the nightstand. "The guests have checked out—all except Mr. Palmer. He decided to stay another day. Oh, and Mr. Ramsey left for New York. He was awfully worried about you, but I convinced him you'd be fine by the time he gets back."

Roseanne had pretended to be sick in Las Vegas, but the morning after their return, she'd spent more time in the bathroom than in bed, and she'd spent *a lot of time* huddled under the covers.

She'd managed to drag herself out of bed the last few days, but this morning, the ailment had returned with a vengeance. Roseanne eyed the food skeptically. "Thank you. What time is it anyway?"

"Almost noon."

"I've got to get up." Roseanne tried to sit up, but her stomach rolled, forcing her to lie back down.

"You don't have to do anything, Ms. Meadows. We've got it covered."

"I hate being useless," she moaned.

"No worries. You just concentrate on getting better. We'll take care of everything else."

"Seriously, I don't know what I'd do without you." Once Ford and Becky's business had taken off, and the rooms at The Yellow Rose were once again full, Roseanne had hired a small staff to take care of the bed-and-breakfast guests, and thank goodness she had; otherwise, she'd be screwed. Kay Rogers was her jack-of-all-trades in charge of making sure the guests' needs were met, and scheduling and supervising the other two new hires—Jamie Higgs, the cook, and

Mary Hernandez, the housekeeper. Roseanne made a mental note to add nurse and surrogate mother to the woman's duties. "You deserve a raise."

"I wouldn't turn it down." The woman bustled around the room, straightening things and picking up dirty clothes. "We'll talk about it when you're back on your feet. In the meantime, don't worry about a thing. I'll stay in one of the empty rooms tonight, just in case you need something."

"You are an angel, Kay."

"I know."

Roseanne smiled at the older woman's spunk. The retired school teacher who had never married had taken the job to supplement her fixed income, and, in her words, to keep from going insane. Years of noisy classrooms hadn't prepared her quiet later years. The last few days, she'd earned every penny of her salary, and then some.

Later, Roseanne managed to sit up and sip the now-cooled tea and nibble on crackers, her thoughts turned to Scott Ramsey. Yes, her illness the last few days would have prevented her from accompanying him to New York, but he could have at least told her about the party. Maybe expressed his dismay that she wasn't up to attending. But he'd said nothing.

Despite the difference in their lives—he was filthy rich and she wasn't—they'd been more than compatible in bed. At times, she'd managed to forget Scott didn't actually live in Butte Plains, that his tenure here was only temporary. She didn't want to admit it, but his sister had been right. Scott had no intention of staying in Texas. Which meant she needed to end the relationship before her heart was beyond the point of no return.

The following day she felt better, and the day after that she was even better—almost her old self. Enough at least to fix a couple of sandwiches and meet Becky at her office for a quick lunch. Her friend usually came to the B&B for their weekly lunch date, but, after being out of town for over a week, she needed to catch up on the paperwork that had accumulated in her absence. Roseanne could relate.

Though Kay did a great job running the B&B, as the owner, there were still things only she could handle. Then there was the cookbook she'd been working on for the last few months. She'd pitched the idea to some big-time agents, and one of them had actually asked to see what she had so far. She couldn't just let that dream go by the wayside. She had more recipes to perfect and agents to query.

For dessert, Roseanne grabbed two muffins left over from breakfast and a thermos of sweet tea and headed out. Becky had been watching for her and came out to help her carry everything in from the car. "I can't thank you enough for doing this," she said, relieving Roseanne of the heavy thermos. "If I'd known taking a couple of extra days for a honeymoon would double my workload when I got back, I'd have told Ford the wedding would have to wait and hightailed it home."

"You know you wouldn't have done any such thing."

"Maybe not, but, in retrospect, it might have been the right thing to do."

Roseanne followed her friend to her office. The stacks of papers on her desk were indeed impressive, but portable. They moved a couple to nearby shelves to make room for their picnic then got down to the business of eating and catching up on everything that had happened in the four days since they'd seen each other.

"What do you mean? You aren't regretting getting married are you?"

Becky waved away Roseanne's concerns. "Not at all. It's just that we should have thought it through, you know?"

"Enlighten me, please? I don't have the foggiest notion what you're talking about." She poured sweet tea into two plastic cups she'd brought along. Becky drank down half of hers and held her cup out for a refill.

"Ford is like Butte Plains' favorite son, or something like that. People, meaning his mother, have expectations for him."

She was beginning to see. Ford's family had been the pinnacle of Butte Plains society for three generations.

Everything they did was news in town. Becky's family didn't run in the same circles, but a mother could be touchy about her only daughter getting married. "And perhaps your mother has expectations for you, too? In terms of a big, splashy wedding with lots of guests and a write-up in the local paper?"

"Yeah, those kind of expectations." She took a big bite of her sandwich, closed her eyes, and moaned as she chewed. "Sweet Lord, what you do to chicken salad, woman. It should be illegal."

Roseanne smiled and took a bite of her sandwich. She did do a good chicken salad, which was why it was going to be one of the recipes featured in her cookbook. "I had extra, so I brought it for you. There's enough for two more sandwiches. Maybe you can figure out how to spread it on bread and then you and Ford can have a picnic lunch tomorrow."

Her friend glared at her for a second before a broad smile broke over her face. "I'm going to ignore that jab at my cooking skills and just say thank you. Though it might be dinner tonight instead of lunch tomorrow. Both of us are buried in paperwork." She swept her hand out to indicate the stacks of folders and papers occupying nearly every flat space in her small office.

"That sucks."

"Sure does. I don't even have time to talk to you about our wedding."

"What's to say? I was there, remember?"

"Oh, not that one. The one we're going to have here."

"Here? As in Butte Plains?"

"Yep. We were hoping we could use your garden at The Yellow Rose. I've got a date picked out." She clicked a couple of keys on her computer and consulted the screen. "Three months from today. How's that work for you?"

Becky had always had a way of talking in shorthand, but this was ridiculous. Roseanne was at least a dozen steps behind in figuring out what her friend was talking about. "Wait. Let me get this straight. You want to have another wedding, three months from now. At my place."

"See, you aren't slow. I don't know what Chucky Bruce was talking about."

Chucky Bruce had been a mean-spirited bully back in fourth grade. His favorite insult was to call someone slow. He'd made the mistake of insulting Roseanne on the playground one day and had paid the price for it. She'd socked him in the nose, proving that at least her fist was faster than his ability to get out of the way. The offended appendage bled like a son of a gun, prompting the school nurse to be called, as well as the principal. Roseanne had taken a three day suspension and a month of helping the cleaning crew after school rather than apologize. Chucky, likewise, had refused to apologize and had received the same suspension and a month of early morning study hall. It seemed he was behind in all his subjects and needed the extra help more than he needed to empty wastebaskets. "Heard he got on with the new waste management company over in

Prairieview."

"I heard the same thing." She crunched a potato chip. "Back to my wedding. I know you're busy, but do you think you could handle most of the arrangements? I'll find a dress. Colin said he'd sing. We'll need a band, a preacher, flowers, cake. What else?"

"Invitations, a photographer, a tent, table and chairs for the reception. A caterer if you plan on serving anything more than cake. And security. If your brother is going to be there, someone will have to keep his adoring fans away." They'd all had the pleasure of seeing Colin perform in Las Vegas. The up-and-coming country music star had a large fan base made up of primarily young women who all wanted to become Mrs. Colin Parker. Who could blame them? He was single, sexy, and successful. And a genuinely nice guy, too.

"See? I knew you were the perfect person to put in charge. You're already thinking of things I never would have. Oh, and can we keep the fact that Ford and I are already married a secret for now?"

"You aren't going to tell anyone?"

Becky shook her head. "Nope. We have the video from Vegas. How cool would it be to show it at the reception?" Her friend smiled. "Let everyone in on the secret then?"

"I think it's an insanely great idea." She clasped Becky's hand. "Maybe the two of you could step out for your first dance when the Elvis impersonator starts to sing 'Love Me Tender.'"

"Oh, wouldn't that be fun?" Becky rocked back in her chair, a wicked grin on her face. "We'd just finished saying our vows, so everyone will know when we step into the spotlight in the center of the dance floor while the Elvis sings on the big screen. It's perfect, Roseanne. Absolutely perfect." She clapped her hands like a child who just found out she was going to Disneyland.

"It will be if I can pull this off in three months."

"I never thought I would say this in my lifetime, but money is no object. I'll establish an account to cover all the expenses, so you won't be out a cent of your own money. You'll have full access to the funds. No need to bother me with the details unless you need more. Then, by all means, let me know and I'll put more in the account."

"You don't want to establish a budget?" Roseanne's parents had plenty of money now, but that hadn't always been the case. Like Becky, she'd grown up pinching pennies until they screamed. Money had not only been an object—it had been a deep chasm without a bridge.

"I'm tempted, but I honestly don't think it's necessary. Do you remember when we used to have pretend weddings in your grandmother's backyard?"

They'd scattered boxes and anything they could find around the walkways for the "guests" to sit on, and used the rose arbor as a backdrop for the ceremony. They'd also gotten in trouble for cutting her grandmother's flowers to use for bouquets for the pretend wedding party. "How many times did we marry that old momma cat off to your Ken doll anyway? A dozen?"

"At least. I still think that garden is one

of the most beautiful places in the entire town. My tastes are simple, and you know that better than anyone. I trust you to create a lovely setting for the ceremony, and another one for the reception. Spend as much as you need, and, for Pete's sake, hire people to do the work. If you're unsure about anything, ask, but I bet you know more about what I'd like than I do."

Roseanne tried to talk Becky into taking a bigger role in the planning, but the woman simply changed the subject. "Have you heard anything from the editor who wanted to see your cookbook?"

She filled her friend in on the latest, which wasn't much, before packing up and leaving Becky to her work. If she was going to pull off a grand wedding in three months, she'd better get moving.

CHAPTER THREE

Scott stood in the foyer of his Manhattan apartment, his gaze taking in the spartan landscape. This used to be home, but it no longer felt like it, if it ever had. The ultra-modern décor seemed cold and uninviting—just the opposite of what the decorator had claimed. He'd been dating the woman for a few weeks when he'd closed on the property. Her references were good—or so his sister had said. He'd been too busy with the design-build company he'd started with Ford to check for himself. If he had, he might have declined her services. But he hadn't, and this was the result. A stark, hard landscape with more sharp edges than a pack of razor blades and not a comfortable place to sit in the entire place.

The apartment had been one of two considered for a spread in a major style magazine, but had lost out to a penthouse owned by some branch of the Saudi royal family. By artist's standards, the place was well-done, he assumed, but by his standards, it looked like a museum where the furniture was the art.

He'd cut the decorator loose shortly after the place was finished and hadn't seen her since. He'd heard through the grapevine she'd finally scored a spot in the magazine. He'd briefly wondered who she'd duped into letting her have her way with their space then promptly forgot all about her again.

He made his way to the master bedroom where he stretched out on the only soft surface in the entire apartment, his bed, and rested one forearm across his eyes. He'd never been so tired in his life. It wasn't the trip weighing him down, but what he'd left behind. As soon as the wheels had left the runway, he'd wished he'd told Roseanne the real reason he had to go to New York, but the opportunity to do so had passed, and telling her after the fact would only make his omission worse.

Dropping his arm, he gazed at the ceiling. A monstrous lighting fixture that looked like someone had run sheet metal through a giant chipper then let a blind man stick all the pieces back together hung disturbingly low. He'd been assured it was as much art as it was functional, but it still gave him the creeps. He much preferred the antique chandelier that hung over his bed at The Yellow Rose. The soft curves of the armatures reminded him of the best parts of a woman's body, and the soft glow from the candle-tipped bulbs bathed everything in soothing gold tones.

Just thinking about his room at the B&B, he could feel the tension leaving his body. He recalled having the same feeling the first day he'd arrived in Texas. The car he'd hired at the airport had sped across wide open plains and crept through small towns, and, with each mile, the tightness in his shoulders had eased until he'd been able to breathe deeply. If he closed his eyes, he could still smell the fresh scent left behind after a passing shower dampened the dusty sidewalks. There was nothing in New York City that could compare with it.

Just like there was nothing that would compare with the independent Texan who had captured his attention and refused to let go. Roseanne Meadows. Her name fit her. As lovely as any bloom in her garden, she was as open and sweet as a meadow in spring.

Scott groaned and sat up, shaking off the memories. What the fuck? The Texas heat must have scrambled his brains. Why else would he be thinking all that poetic shit about a woman? Maybe the command performance for his mother was a good thing. A couple of days in the Big Apple, and he'd have his perspective back then he could return to Butte Plains, hire someone to run the leather goods factory he'd purchased. In a few weeks, a month tops, he'd be back here for good. In the meantime, he'd hire someone to gut this place. Once he was back for good, he'd decorate it himself.

Scott checked his watch. He had just enough time to shower and dress before he was supposed to meet his sister in the lobby of their building.

His mother had requested his presence tonight at a party to celebrate his parents' thirty-fifth wedding anniversary. Professional excuse maker that he'd become, he couldn't think of a single legitimate reason to miss the affair. If nothing else, he'd be there to show support for his dad. The man deserved some kind of award for putting up with Scott's mother for thirty-plus years. The woman took meddling to a whole new level. Hell, she'd practically made a career out of sticking her nose in other people's business.

Checking his appearance one last time, he picked up the wrapped gifts for the celebrants and made his way down to the lobby where he'd agreed to meet his sister who lived two floors below his penthouse apartment. Expecting to be kept waiting, he was surprised to find her flirting with the new guy, Alan, he thought, at the security desk. The poor kid appeared to be in shock. Who could blame him? Dressed to impress, as always, Ronnie sparkled from head to toe.

"Come on, Ronnie," he said, brushing his fingers over her arm to drag her attention away from the younger man. "We're going to be late."

The doorman anticipated their leaving and held the heavy glass panel open for them. Scott stopped short and waited for Veronica to say her good-byes. When she sailed past him on impossibly high heels and a cloud of expensive perfume, he fell into step behind her. "You didn't get Mom and Dad a present?"

"I'm not an idiot, Snotty Scotty. Of course I did. Raymond put it in the car already."

"How many times do I have to tell you not to call me that?" Scott nodded at his driver who stood next to the limo he rarely used. He preferred the SUV around the city, but the drive out to the Hamptons called for more luxury.

Besides, his sister refused to ride in his SUV.

"You'll always be a snot, big brother." She failed to acknowledge the man holding the back door open for her as she ducked into the car.

"Thanks, Raymond." Scott shook hands with his driver. He was one of several the Ramsey family kept on the payroll so no one would ever have to drive anywhere if they didn't want to, and most of his family would rather stay home than be seen driving themselves anywhere. "How's Margaret?"

"The missus is doing just fine, sir. Looking forward to retiring next year."

"That's awesome. She teaches third grade, doesn't she?"

"Yes, sir."

"I don't know how she does it."

"Me, either, but she loves the kids. I think she remembers every one she's ever taught, too."

Scott smiled, thinking of the kind, older woman who had taught him when he was that age. "And no doubt they all remember her, too. I know I'll never forget her."

"I'll tell her you said so, sir."

Dreading the next several hours, Scott climbed in behind Veronica and settled in as Raymond closed the door and made his way around to the driver's seat. A long, narrow box occupied the back facing seat. "Seriously? You got them flowers?"

Ronnie shrugged. "Pink roses. You know how much Mom loves them."

"Mom does, but this is Dad's anniversary, too, you know?" He shook his head. He should have known Ronnie wouldn't give more than a moment's thought to selecting a gift for the occasion. If it wasn't about her, she couldn't be bothered.

"They've got *everything* they could possibly want." She eyed the two small boxes he'd placed beside her gift. "You got them jewelry? How original."

"It's not like I sent my secretary to pick something out. I designed these myself and had them made." He hadn't been sure the jeweler in Butte Plains would be up to the task, but he'd taken a chance and hadn't been disappointed. The man had been in business there for decades, a tribute to his skills, but the downturn in the economy had forced him to reduce his inventory to the lowest price point possible. He'd been grateful for the business, and Scott had been happy to help the old guy out.

Ronnie picked invisible lint from her dress. "Show off. You're such an ass-kisser."

He shrugged and kept his mouth shut. He loved his sister, but take away the shared bloodline, and he doubted they would be friends. He might be an ass-kisser, but to his mind that beat expecting everyone to bow down to him. Less than two weeks ago, she'd shown up in Las Vegas with one of Ford's major competitors in the sex toy market and done her best to convince Becky that Ford had agreed to sell out. It had almost worked. Would have if Becky hadn't seen through the charade. Instead of breaking the couple up, which was Ronnie's goal, she'd forced them together. Thus the hasty wedding at the Elvis is King

Wedding Chapel. Yeah, his sister was a piece of work.

"I'm surprised you didn't bring that little mouse you've been seeing. I'm sure she'd fit in just fine."

Every muscle in his body tensed at the sarcasm oozing from her words. "What do you mean by that?"

Ronnie's laugh was pure evil. "You've got nothing in common with her, that's what I mean. She's a hick who runs a bed-and-breakfast, for heaven's sake. Her idea of a party is paper plates and red plastic cups and beer straight from the bottle. I saw the way she dresses." She shivered. "Where'd she get that getup she had on in Vegas? A thrift store? All I can say is she must be something in bed, that's the only reason I can think of for you to be seeing her."

Scott balled his hands into fists. His sister was the last person on earth who should be criticizing another, especially someone like Roseanne. "My personal life is none of your business, and just because she wasn't born wearing a designer outfit doesn't mean anything.

She lives within her means, and even if she had all the money in the world, she wouldn't throw it away on overpriced clothes and meaningless parties. And for the record, there's nothing like a cold beer straight from the bottle."

"You're a Neanderthal."

"You're a bitch."

"I'm going to tell Mom you said that."

"Grow up, Ronnie." He turned to stare out the window. It was going to be a long ride.

Curtis, who had been the butler for the Ramsey family as long as Scott could recall, greeted them at the door and directed them to the back of the house where all the guests were assembled. His mother had thrown open the glass partitions separating the indoor and outdoor living spaces, creating one giant area for partygoers to mix and mingle. He left the gifts he'd brought with Curtis and made his way through the already-substantial crowd, searching for the happy couple. Several bars were set up around the perimeter of the terrace. Scott stopped long enough to obtain what he expected would be the first of many drinks he would consume before the night was over. While the bartender mixed the drink he'd requested, Scott continued to scan the crowd. He wanted to find his folks, but he likened attending these kinds of events to a soldier walking into an enemy stronghold with his buddies. Friends were easy enough to identify, but that left everyone else in question. He'd already spotted half a dozen women close to his age. Most were the unmarried daughters of his parents' friends, but there were a few new faces, too. Best to steer clear of them, just in case.

He'd parted ways with Ronnie the second they set foot inside the house, but as he turned to scoop up the scotch and soda the bartender placed near his elbow, he caught sight of his sister and a woman he'd never seen before. Angled away from the masses, the two stood close together and appeared to be deep in conversation. Scott brought the glass to his lips and sipped. Did he even want to know what she was up to? Probably not.

"Well, well. If it isn't the prodigal son." A heavy hand clamped his shoulder. Scott smiled and turned to greet the man of the hour. Gerald Ramsey had aged well. A tad over six feet tall, he had broad shoulders and the blond hair Scott had inherited still hadn't given way to gray. Daily tennis matches kept his body in shape and his skin tan.

"Dad." He clapped his father on the shoulder. "Congratulations."

"It's good to see you, son." The elder man gave his son a pat on the back. He'd never been one to hug his children or show much emotion. Strange, Scott thought as his paternal grandparents had been the exact opposite. Both had been easy with their affections. "Save your congratulations for your mother. How she's put up with me all these years, I'll never know."

"And here I thought it was the other way around," Scott said, half joking.

His father pointed to the glass in Scott's hand then said to the bartender, "I'll have one of those." Then he turned his attention back to his son. "I mean it. It's good to see you. When are you going to come to your senses and come back home?"

"I don't know. Never, maybe." Might as well get it out in the open. Plant the seed and let it sprout.

"You can't be serious." His father's expression remained blank. *Never let them see your drama.* That was always Gerald Ramsey's excuse for avoiding talking about anything serious in a public gathering. He took a sip of his drink. "Is it that woman, the innkeeper that Veronica told us about?"

A ripple of unease crept across his skin. "What did Ronnie say?"

"Not much. Just that you were seeing some working girl down there. Slumming, she said."

I'll kill her. His meddling sister had gone too far. She needed to keep her nose out of other people's business and her mouth shut. "You make it sound like Roseanne hangs out on street corners. She owns a bed-and-breakfast. Yes, she works, but most people do. It's not anything to be ashamed of."

"Didn't say it was, just that this woman is beneath you."

Scott was having a hard time keeping his expression neutral in the face of such absurdity. He clenched his jaw tight and held onto his drink with both hands to keep himself steady. "You've got that wrong. She's way out of my league. Unlike me, she started with nothing and built a successful business that has weathered a huge economic downturn. She's smart and resourceful and not afraid to get her hands dirty. Nothing I've done can compare to what she's accomplished."

"All I'm saying, son, is that you and this woman don't have anything in common. Go ahead, get your fill of her then come back home and settle down with someone more fitting. Make your mother happy and give her some grandbabies." Before Scott could reply, his father said, "Now, if you'll excuse me, I've got to get back to the party before June sends out the search and rescue team. Remember what I said, son. We're counting on you."

Scott watched his dad's tuxedo-clad back disappear into the crowd hovering just inside the open doors leading to the great room. His gaze drifted to the spot he'd last seen his sister. A trio of older couples now occupied the space, smiling politely at a conversation he knew by heart. No one at these things spoke about anything of consequence. Society chitchat. The weather. So-and-so's polo match. Their latest trip to fill-in-the-blank European city. Surrounded by people, he felt alone. He always had—until he'd met Ford Adams freshman year at MIT. His college roommate had never thought Scott was weird because he wanted to do something with his life besides find creative ways to piss away money. The endless balls, parties, and fundraisers had always seemed pointless to the Ramsey's oldest child. He'd rather draw some fantastical invention or take something apart and put it back together than drink and socialize with a bunch of people who had to hire someone to entertain them. And he'd never understood the need for fundraisers. Why pay to go to an event when you could simply donate the same amount of money to the group or foundation in need? He'd heard once about a cause that had sent out invitations to an un-ball. Invitees were asked to purchase tickets for a ball that would never happen. No money was spent on a fancy location or over-the-top decorations. No party planner was needed. No band or DJ was hired. No one had to spend money on a gown or new shoes or to have their hair and nails done. Every cent of the money collected from ticket sales went directly to the organization the nonevent was created to help. Scott had gladly donated a huge sum from his personal account. That's the way fundraising should be.

This glittery party scene wasn't him. It never had been. He tugged on his collar and tried to swallow his distaste at the life he'd been born into. His blood might be blue, but he'd never felt like he belonged among these people. An image popped into his head—his best friend, Ford Adams—working to save his family's business, and loving every minute of it. Designing. Creating. Building something with his intellect, if not his hands.

Then there was Roseanne Meadows. Things were better for her now with Ford and Becky's business bringing people to town, but, being a true entrepreneur, Roseanne was exploring other income streams. He'd seen the notes she kept for the cookbook she wanted to publish. Life had given her lemons, and, instead of folding, she'd made lemon pound cake.

His gaze drifted over the carefully chosen guests. He saw a handful he judged to be happy, and a whole lot more he figured were absolutely miserable based on what he knew of their lives. The vast majority he guessed were just living each day, much like himself, not unhappy.

Was that all he could say for himself? That he wasn't unhappy? *Shit.* How had that happened?

"Scott!" He turned toward the voice so familiar to him. "Gerald said he'd seen you."

"Hi, Mom." June Ramsey never went anywhere, not even to the breakfast nook in her own kitchen without looking her best. For her thirty-fifth anniversary, she'd chosen a floor-length gown in muted gold that made her tan look deeper and her brown eyes sparkle. The cost of her dress alone would probably feed a family of four for a year or more. Weekly trips to the spa and a strict regime kept her looking a good ten years younger than her actual age. She'd never forgive him for messing up her makeup, so he smiled and kissed the air near her cheek. "Happy Anniversary."

"It's good to see you." She studied his face like it was a painting she wasn't sure she wanted to purchase. "You look tired. Is everything okay?"

No. No, it's not. The conversation he'd had with his father had left him on edge. If his mother mentioned anything about Roseanne being unsuitable, he wasn't sure he could keep from causing a scene. Not that he cared what any of his parents' friends thought about him, but there was just enough blue blood in his veins to make him think twice before he ruined his parents' party. He silently thanked the universe, and his mother, for providing the perfect excuse to get the hell out of there. "I'm feeling a little under the weather," he lied, "but I had to come and wish you and Dad another thirty-five years."

"I'm so glad you came, but maybe you should go home, get some rest."

Home. Wherever the hell that was. "I think I will, if you don't mind?"

"Not at all. Did Veronica come with you?"

He glanced over his mother's head. "She's here somewhere. I can send my car back for her."

"Nonsense." She waved his offer off. "We'll make sure she gets home, or she can stay the night."

He hugged her to him, placed another air kiss to her temple. "Love you, Mom. I'll see you soon."

"Love you, too."

As soon as he stepped inside his apartment, he knew he couldn't stay there a minute longer than necessary. It was late, but having boatloads of money meant doors were open to you around the clock. He pulled out his cell phone, scrolled through his contacts until he found the one he wanted. A few minutes later, he was tossing clothes in a suitcase, preparing to head back to Texas, and what he hoped was his future.

CHAPTER FOUR

"You're back."

"I said I would be. You haven't rented my room out to someone else have you?" Scott set his suitcase in the wide foyer of the B&B and smiled at the owner of the inn who wasn't smiling back at him.

"No. I haven't, but maybe I should."

He stood frozen, one hand on the handle of his luggage, the other in his pocket where he'd deposited his keys. What the hell had happened while he was gone? "What are you saying? You want me to leave?"

Roseanne glanced over her shoulder in the direction of the kitchen then back at him. "Keep your voice down. The whole world doesn't need to know our business."

Scott didn't care who heard, but appearances meant a lot to Roseanne, so he lowered his voice to a near whisper. "What's going on?" For the first time since he'd entered the house, he noticed she was wringing her hands—something she only did when she was nervous.

"Did you think I wouldn't find out?"

He cocked his head to one side. "Find out what?"

"Your parents' anniversary party?" She quit fidgeting and squared her shoulders. Her hands became small fists at her sides. "You know—the one you attended last night?"

Scott sighed and dropped his gaze to the floor. *Shit.* What could he say? *I didn't want to drag you into the mess that is my family? I didn't want you to meet my parents? I didn't want you to get hurt?* All of them true, but obviously not what she wanted to hear, so he pulled out the only plausible explanation he could think of. "You were sick. I thought knowing what you were missing would make you feel even worse."

Her face turned thunderous. "That's bullshit, and you know it. You knew about the party long before I got sick. You could have told me anytime, but you didn't because you didn't want me to go with you. I'm not an idiot, Scott. I know I'm not in your league, but you could have been honest with me. I deserved that much."

"I wanted—"

She held her hand up. "Stop. Just stop. Don't say another word. I have no right to be upset, but I am, which is on me. I let myself think there was more between us than there was. So, thanks for the reality check, and please find another place to stay as soon as possible."

He should have told her about the party when he first heard about it. Roseanne was more than capable of holding her own in his parents' world. A cold, hard truth settled over him. Yes, he'd been protecting her from the pointed barbs his family could throw, but he'd also been protecting himself. He didn't want Roseanne to see the way his family treated him. Didn't want her to know he was, if not exactly the black sheep, the one with the purple stripes—the one his family couldn't understand. Had never made an effort to understand. He'd screwed up, big time. Worse, he had no idea how to fix it. "You can't be serious."

Her features hardened even more, and he got a sick feeling in the pit of his stomach. He'd said the wrong thing. As usual. "I've never been more serious in my life. You've got twenty-four hours. If you aren't out by then, you'll find your things waiting for you on the front porch. Is that clear?"

His mouth had done enough for one day, so he simply nodded.

"Good. We're done." She turned and disappeared into her office. The soft click of her door closing might as well have been the clang of a cell door for the finality of it.

He took the stairs two at a time to his second-story room. It took only a few minutes to toss his things into the duffel bag he'd stuffed beneath the bed. As he looked around the room to make sure he hadn't missed anything, a deep sense of sadness overtook him. Funny, he'd called this place home for a few short months, but had felt absolutely nothing when he'd left the Manhattan apartment he'd lived in for years. He couldn't leave without one last look out the window overlooking the back gardens. His New York apartment had spectacular views, but they were nothing compared to this. The colorful blooms seemed random, but were anything but. They required careful attention which Roseanne lovingly gave them, just as she did everything she did. Whether it was her grandmother's home she'd converted to a bed-and-breakfast, or the cookbook she was working on, or the local civic committees she served on. Everything she did, she did with love.

Did she love him? He'd thought so. She wasn't the type to give herself to a man she didn't have feelings for, and she'd given him everything in bed. The thought of not feeling her skin against his again, of not sinking into her welcoming body, or experiencing the high he felt when she found her pleasure made him wish he could turn back time. Where was a do-over when you needed it?

As he gazed out the window, the old orange tabby cat Roseanne had befriended wandered onto the gravel path in the direction of the back porch where he knew the feline would find a bowl of fresh water and kibble. It had taken weeks to win the cat's trust, but Roseanne had patiently waited for the feline to venture close enough she could touch her. He'd witnessed the process from this very window, falling under the woman's spell the same as the cat had. And like the orange ball of fur, he had no intention of going anywhere.

Butte Plains was his home now. He'd made that decision almost as soon as the jet's wheels had left the ground in New York. There was nothing for him there. Everything he wanted was here, including Roseanne. He'd honor her wishes and find another place to live, but if she thought she'd seen the last of him, she had another think coming. He'd take a page from her own book and win her back with patience and persistence.

~ ~ ~

Roseanne closed the office door and leaned back against it. The last thing she wanted was for Scott to see her crying. He'd treated their relationship like it was nothing, and she didn't want him to know how much that hurt. Her pain was hers, and, like most things in her life, she preferred to keep it private.

That didn't mean it didn't hurt like hell, though. Secure behind the locked door, she sank to the floor and let the tears fall. She'd been a fool to let herself fall in love with a guest. She'd been a fool to fall into his bed, too. He'd been a generous lover, and though she didn't have a lot of experience for comparison sake, he'd more than satisfied her. With him, she'd comfortably explored her sexuality and learned what really turned her on. She doubted she'd ever find another man who made her feel the way Scott did.

She'd let the good times they'd had together blind her to reality. They were worlds apart everywhere but the bedroom. She ran a B&B in a small west

Texas town, and he was a billionaire with several businesses and a home in New York. She'd never even been to New York. Her family had never been what she'd call rich. Well-to-do by most standards. Her father was a lawyer and made enough to allow her mother be a stay-at-home mom. They'd had expectations for their only child, expectations she could never meet. Law school had never been her deal. She'd tried and tried to convince them she just wasn't cut out for contracts and legal briefs, but all they'd heard was rebellion. God bless her grandmother's soul, but her passing had provided Roseanne with an opportunity she had grabbed with both hands. She could still hear her father's calm voice telling her she was on her own. "Don't come crying to us for money when this crazy scheme of yours fails. We won't bail you out." Even at her lowest point during the economic downturn, when her financial situation couldn't have looked bleaker, she hadn't even thought of asking them for help. She'd cut expenses, worked her fingers to the bone, and held on until, thankfully, things had started to look up.

Then in walked Scott Ramsey. He'd turned her world upside down. An ill-advised fling with a guest. Another detour in her otherwise orderly life.

Well, she was back on the main road now. If she wasn't good enough for the Ramseys, well, screw them. Though she dearly would have loved to see their faces when they realized their precious son's date was an innkeeper from Butt Plug, Texas! That brought tears of mirth to her eyes. She swiped them away with a sigh.

Reality sucked. She'd been living in a romance novel. But no more. She wasn't Elizabeth Bennett, and Scott wasn't Mr. Darcy. It was time to dry her eyes and get on with life. Maybe someday she'd meet a man who dwelled on her social plane, who loved her for who she was, and would encourage her to explore her slightly kinky side the way Scott had. If not, she'd at least find fulfillment in her work.

That wasn't a four letter word in her

vocabulary. She'd always found satisfaction in a job well-done, whether it was tending to the plants her grandparents had lovingly planted, or perfecting a recipe, or simply changing a light bulb. The finished product justified the labor put into the project.

She wiped her wet cheeks on her sleeve then hauled herself off the floor. Her heart ached even more than her throat, which was raw from crying, but both would heal. One sooner than the other, but time healed all wounds, or so they said. Straightening her clothes, she ventured to her new ergonomic desk chair. No sooner had her butt hit the cushioned bottom than her phone rang. She glanced at the blinking light. Her private line. She cleared her throat and pasted on a smile, hoping the physical act of appearing happy would carry over to the words spilling from her mouth. "Hello?"

"What the heck is going on, Roseanne?" Becky Parker-Adams screamed at her.

"Going on?"

"Don't play ignorant with me. Scott just called Ford, wanting to know if he could move into the Adams's gatehouse."

Though it was meant to be servants' quarters, the gatehouse was still one of the largest private dwellings in Butte Plains, and much more modern than The Yellow Rose. Scott would probably feel right at home there. "Is there a problem with him staying there? Ford moved in with you, didn't he?" Rather than stay in the family mansion, Ford had opted to bunk in the gatehouse when he'd come home for his father's funeral. When his stay in town had been extended, he'd opted to stay put. Since Ford and Becky were keeping their Vegas nuptials a secret, he'd quietly moved into Becky's house while maintaining the appearance that he was still living there.

"Of course there's not a problem with him staying there, but there is a problem with him not staying with you. What happened?"

Roseanne knew this conversation would have to take place eventually, but she'd hoped it would be a while before her best friend learned Scott had moved out. She should have guessed he'd call on *his* best friend to solve his temporary housing problem. The best she could hope for was to go with a bit of the truth and save the whole story for a time when it wouldn't hurt so much to tell it. She sighed and dropped her forehead to the desk blotter. "I needed the room, so I asked him to leave. You know I don't rent long-term. He's been here for months. This is an inn, not a boarding house."

"Yes, but—"

"But nothing, Becks." She sat up and pulled the nearest file front and center. "Look, can we not talk about this now? I have a zillion things that need to be done today, and I know you do, too."

"Do you need me to come over?"

She hated the concern in her friend's voice. She felt foolish enough as it was. The last thing she needed to do was confess to Becky that she'd been living a fantasy, dreaming of finding love in the Yankee's arms. No, that was something she'd prefer to keep to herself. At least until her heart scabbed over. Maybe then she'd confide in her best friend. "No. I'm fine. Really."

A long sigh slid across the phone line. "I thought you two were such a cute couple."

"We had some fun together, but we're adults and we have to come in off the playground sometime. Turns out that's today."

After a long silence, Becky said, "You know this conversation isn't over, don't you?"

"I know. Give me a few days, okay?"

"You have until our lunch on Wednesday and not a minute longer. Do you hear me?"

"I hear you. Maybe we could meet somewhere neutral. I don't want anyone else to hear this."

Appeased by her agreement to spill all, Becky suggested a diner that had just opened out on the interstate. The place was noisy and catered to motorists rather than locals. Chances of them meeting anyone they knew were slim, making it the perfect place for a girlfriend chat. Roseanne agreed to the location and,

after assuring Becky she was fine, ended
the call.

CHAPTER FIVE

It had been forty-two hours and eleven minutes since she'd sent Scott packing, and her heart still felt as if she'd jabbed a knife in it. The worst part was, every time she thought about the man she loved, it was as if she grabbed the handle and gave the weapon a savage twist. At times, she thought the pain would bring her to her knees, but she'd miraculously remained on her feet. Despite her resolve to get on with her life, she'd cried enough to risk serious dehydration.

When the waitress came to take their drink orders, Roseanne requested a pitcher of water. Becky raised one eyebrow—a promise to get to the bottom of her action—then asked for a glass of sweet tea.

As soon as the waitress went to fill their orders, Becky dove in. She leaned forward, arms folded on the table. "A pitcher of water?"

"I need to hydrate. It's hot outside, if you haven't noticed."

"It's not that hot."

"There are other things that can cause dehydration, you know."

The waitress returned. As she placed their drinks on the table, Becky kept her gaze on Roseanne. Her friend was too astute to miss the bags under her eyes or the red rimming her eyelids. She'd tried to hide both, but drugstore makeup could only do so much. Heck, she doubted the stage makeup Becky used when she taped her television show would be a match for her tear-ravaged face.

"A sweet tea and a pitcher of water. Are you ladies ready to order, or should I give you a minute?"

Neither one of them had picked up a menu yet. They did so now, taking the laminated pages from a rack next to the wall and perusing them.

"I'll be back in a minute. Take your time."

Roseanne closed her menu. Her appetite had wavered from nonexistent to insatiable the last few days. She chalked it up to her recent illness coupled with bouts of crying. Becky looked the whole menu over twice before setting it aside. Taking the cue, the waitress reappeared, pad in hand.

"I'll have the double cheeseburger and a side of fries," Becky said.

Roseanne ordered the chicken noodle soup and extra crackers, earning another look from her lunch partner. "What?" she said when the waitress departed.

"You're on a liquid diet?"

"No. I'm just not very hungry. I had a big breakfast." Actually, she'd had dry toast and a few sips of hot tea, and even that hadn't stayed down. Darned stomach. Life's upsets had always affected her physically, but not to this extent. For both her physical and mental well-being, she had to get over Scott Ramsey's betrayal. If talking about it with

Becky would help, she was all for it.

"Want to know what I think?"

Roseanne picked up the pitcher and poured herself a glass of ice water. "Not particularly, but you're going to tell me anyway, aren't you?"

"You know I am, girlfriend. That's what friends are for, aren't they?"

Roseanne shrugged and took a big swig. The cold drink instantly made her head ache and her stomach churn. Damn, why hadn't she asked for some bread to nibble on or something? She placed one hand on her stomach and then clamped the other to her forehead, putting pressure on her temples. "If you say so, Becks." There was no use in arguing. Becky couldn't keep her opinion to herself if it was the only thing keeping her from falling off a cliff.

Her friend leaned across the table and whispered, "I think you're pregnant."

Roseanne's head came up so fast she thought it might explode. Becky sat across from her, a Cheshire cat grin on her face. "Are you insane?"

Becky shook her head, the tips of her

high ponytail swishing over one shoulder then the other. "Nope. Tell me it's not true."

Roseanne stared at her friend while the possibility whistled through her head like a freight train bearing down on an unprotected crossing. Moments in time played across her mind—moments spent with Scott. They'd always used protection. *Always.* But nothing short of abstinence was 100 percent, and abstinence had not been something they adhered to. Far from it. They'd made love often up until that last day in Las Vegas.

"I can't be." Even she could hear the doubt in her voice. Becky didn't miss it, either.

"You're going to have to do better than that." Her friend sat back, crossing her arms. Roseanne didn't have to see it to know she'd also crossed her legs. The woman smelled victory.

Roseanne reached for her water, but her hand shook too much, so she set the plastic glass down rather than spill the contents all over herself. "We weren't reckless. We used protection."

"They covered that subject in our sex-ed class in junior high. You were there. I sat next to you."

"I know." The class had been eye-opening and embarrassing. They'd giggled about it for months, speculating on what it would be like to have a guy put his "thing" inside you. Becoming pregnant had been a distant and unreal possibility overshadowed by the process that they'd all but ignored it in their girlish excitement. "The only way to be positive you won't become pregnant is to abstain," she quoted in her best imitation of their teacher, Mrs. Roach.

"Did you abstain?" Becky asked.

Roseanne glared at her companion. "What do you think?"

"I think you and Scott were getting it on like bunnies. Every time I saw the two of you together you couldn't keep your hands off each other."

"That doesn't mean I'm preg...pregnant."

"It doesn't mean you aren't, either."

The waitress returned with their meals. Roseanne took one whiff of the food and excused herself. She made it to the restroom in time, emptied the meager contents of her stomach into the toilet then stared at her reflection in the mirror as she cleaned up afterward. She'd been so busy being mad at Scott for not asking her to go to his parents' party she'd ignored the signs. Could her recent illness be morning sickness? Did that last all day? Did it come and go?

She patted her face with a damp towel. The nausea had dissipated only to be replaced by a gnawing hunger she was afraid the soup she'd ordered wouldn't quench. She crumpled the towel in her fist and tossed it in the trash receptacle. Taking a dry towel from the dispenser, she used it to open the door then tossed it in the wastebasket as she exited the ladies' room. Becky was halfway through with her burger when Roseanne slid into her side of the booth.

"You okay?"

"Yeah. I'm starving." She ladled soup into her mouth as fast as she could without actually drinking it from the bowl. As she'd suspected, the light meal wasn't going to cut it. She eyed the mountain of fries Becky had barely touched.

Becky took her burger then shoved the plate across the table. "Help yourself."

"Thanks." She ate like she hadn't eaten in a week while Becky slowly finished her burger. To her friend's credit, she kept her mouth shut until they'd paid and were standing beside their cars in the parking lot.

"When do you want to take the test?"

Never. "Can we stop at the super store at the next exit? If I buy one at Harrington's Pharmacy, everyone in town will know before I get the box open." The local drugstore was handy, but the clerks were the worst gossips in Butte Plains.

"Remember when Billy Proctor had ringworm?" Becky smiled. "Man, that news spread like wildfire."

Roseanne shuddered. "If you think that spread fast, you can imagine how fast this would hit the grapevine."

"Fiber optic technology has nothing on the Butte Plains grapevine."

"So, can we go to the big, anonymous super store?"

"Lead the way, girlfriend. We can use the self-checkout, too. Only the two of us will know."

~ ~ ~

"It's going to be all right, Roseanne." The uncertainty in Becky's tone said otherwise.

Roseanne stared at the little stick that spelled her doom. *No. No, it isn't.* Nothing was ever going to be all right again.

"Scott will do what's right. He's a good man."

Ah, Becky. Your optimism is showing. If there was one thing Roseanne was certain of, it was that she couldn't tell Scott Ramsey. At least not right away. If he stayed in town there'd be no way to keep him from finding out, and chances were Ford would tell him, too. She couldn't expect Becky to keep the information a secret from her husband forever, and, in turn, he'd feel obligated to tell his best friend. "You're putting too much faith in the man, Becks. He had the chance to take me to meet his parents and he didn't even tell me about it."

"What?"

She sat on the closed toilet seat and waved Becky to the rim of the tub then she proceeded to tell her friend what had led to her kicking Scott out of his room at The Yellow Rose.

"This is different, Roseanne. He didn't tell you about a party. You can't seriously contemplate not telling him he's going to be a father."

"He'll find out soon enough, but please, can you keep this to yourself for a while? I need some time to get used to the idea of being a single mom. I've got to figure out how I'm going to provide for this baby."

"Scott's a billionaire. He'll provide for you and the baby."

"I don't want his money. I don't want him staying in Butte Plains because I'm pregnant. He'll go back to New York in a few months…then I'll tell him."

"I don't like it, but as long as you promise to tell him before the baby is born…"

Roseanne crossed her fingers behind

her back. "I promise."

CHAPTER SIX

Ford waved the bartender over and ordered two beers, one for him, and one for his best friend who looked as if he'd been sucker punched. He'd never seen Scott Ramsey so depressed. At MIT, his roommate had been known as Smiley, while Ford had often been called Grumpy. The man just didn't have it in him to be down. Or so Ford thought.

"Here. Maybe this will help."

"A legal depressant?" Scott took the offered bottle and drank half of it in one draw. "Can't hurt. Thanks."

"I appreciate you staying in the gatehouse. You don't mind driving my car, do you?"

"Nope. It's a nice ride. You sure your mother won't figure out it's me living there and not you?"

Ford took a sip from his beer. "She won't. I've been living there for months and she hasn't come down the drive to see me. If she wants me, she calls and demands my presence at the house. Just don't answer the house phone, and she'll never know."

"Okay, if you say so, but don't you think it would be easier to just tell her you got married? You're going to have a big shindig anyway, so why would she care?"

"I'm her only child. She's been dreaming about my wedding since I was in diapers."

"I hear you. Mine didn't start that early, but she's making up for it now. If she even sees me with an eligible woman, she starts talking about the china and silver patterns she has stored in the attic." He didn't want to dwell on the fact his parents wouldn't see Roseanne as eligible. His mother certainly wouldn't drag out his grandmother's china for a woman who worked to support herself.

Ford signaled the bartender for two more. "Is that why you didn't take Roseanne to their anniversary party?"

"Partly, I guess."

"How do you think she found out about it, anyway?" He'd already heard the story about Scott getting kicked out of the B&B because he hadn't told Roseanne the real reason he went to New York.

"I assumed Becky mentioned it to her."

"Nope. At least I don't think so. I was invited, as you know, but I forgot to mention it to her, so don't you go and tell her or I'll be sharing the gatehouse with you."

Scott shook his head. "She won't hear it from me." He accepted a fresh bottle from the waitress the bartender sent over and handed her his empty. "So, if none of us told her, how did she find out?"

"Did an invite come to the B&B?"

"Nope. Mom sent it to the leather factory. It's the only address she has for me here."

"Leave it lying around in your room?"

"Nope. It's still in my desk drawer at

the factory."

"I don't suppose Roseanne had any reason to go there and snoop around?"

"I can't imagine why she would. Besides, she's as busy as a cab driver on New Year's Eve. The woman has more going on than any of my mother or sister's high society friends."

They drank their beers and contemplated the problem for a few minutes. Ford finally broke the silence. "Did she see your sister in Las Vegas?"

"Not that I know of, but now that you mention it, she acted funny toward me that last day there."

"The same day Ronnie butted into mine and Becky's business?"

"Yeah. The same day." He took a long draw on his beer. "You don't suppose she got to Roseanne that same day, do you?"

"I wouldn't put anything past your sister. She went above and beyond to try to come between me and Becky, and tried to weasel our company out from under us." He shrugged. "I could believe she spread her poison to your girlfriend."

The conversation he'd had with

Ronnie in the limo last week came back to him. "Shit."

"What?"

"Ronnie said some things to me about Roseanne last week on the way out to the estate. I wrote it off as my sister being the bitch she is, but now that I think about it, I wonder if she did have a hand in this."

"Like I said. I wouldn't put it past her, especially after what she did to me and Becky in Vegas." He drained his first beer and started on his second. "I can't believe I dated that woman. What was I thinking?"

"Don't ask me. I never understood what you saw in her."

"You should have said something."

"Would you have listened?"

"Probably not," Ford conceded. "The important thing is that our friendship survived my time with your sister."

"I had faith you'd come around."

"What are you going to do about Roseanne? Are you going to give up on her?"

Scott shook his head. "Can't."

"Yeah, I know how that feels." Ford

eyed the content level then took another swig from his beer. "You have a plan?"

"Not really. I've got a few things to prove to her, I guess."

"Like what?"

"Like I plan to stay here for good."

Ford's right eyebrow raised. "Do you?"

Scott nodded. "I do. This place grows on you."

"And Roseanne is here."

"And Roseanne is here," Scott conceded. "She'd be miserable in New York, and if I'm being honest, I was, too. I like it here. I've got room to breathe."

"I used to think all that room to breathe was the same thing as a long road with a dead end in the middle of nowhere."

"It's not. It's opportunity and space to grow. I won't say it isn't a challenge, because it is, but I was so busy staying alive in the city that I didn't have time to explore the things that made me happy. I can make a difference here. This place needs someone with time and money, and I've got both."

"You're going into philanthropy?"

"Not so much philanthropy as entrepreneurship." He drained his bottle and held it up until the waitress saw and nodded. "Roseanne's on a couple of local committees that could use some help." Another round arrived, and they both took the time to sample the cold brews.

"Details?"

Scott leaned in, resting his forearms on the table. "You know that block of empty buildings downtown? The one where the old Cotton Exchange is?" His friend nodded. "I'm going to buy it. I'll set up my office in one of the buildings and rent out the rest."

"Where are you going to find people to rent to? We've seen a lot of growth in the last few months, but everyone wants new construction closer to the freeway."

"As a matter of fact, I was thinking it might be time to relocate our design-for-hire business from New York to Butte Plains. That way we could keep an eye on it. I've already talked to Riley about moving. Fortunately for us, he's between sugar daddies and thinks some Texas scenery might be just the thing. He made some comment about ranchers, cowboy boots, and Stetsons. I didn't ask any questions, just told him I'd discuss it with you and let him know."

"What about the new designer we hired?"

"He wasn't as eager to load up his covered wagon, but he didn't say absolutely no."

"Then I say we do it. Move the whole thing here. If we have to hire a new designer or two, so be it." Ford and Scott clinked their beer bottles together, sealing the deal. "So, your plan to win Roseanne's affections is to move here and become a land baron?"

"It's the only plan I've got. She doesn't believe I'm going to stay. What says permanent resident better than becoming a major land owner?"

"How about a house? Don't get me wrong. You can stay at the gatehouse as long as you want, but it's not the same as putting down roots."

"Got that covered. I put an offer in on that crumbling Victorian around the corner from Roseanne's place."

"Good Lord! I hope you plan to bulldoze it before it falls in on itself."

"Nope. I admit, it's in worse shape than the one you bought and renovated in New York. I've already spoken to a renovation expert in Dallas about fixing it up."

"I can't even imagine how much that would cost."

"More than I'll be paying for the property. I had it checked out. The foundation is solid, and the basic structure is sound. It was built to last, apparently. Decades of neglect have taken a toll, but it can be saved."

"I'll take your word for it. It's too much house for us, anyway, and we're too busy to oversee a renovation of any kind right now. Becky's house is small, but we're content."

"Compared to the houses you and I grew up in, the crumbling Victorian is tiny, but I suspect it will be big enough for the four or five kids I imagine."

"Whoa!" Ford reared back. "You're talking about having a brood with Roseanne, and the woman isn't even speaking to you? You've got balls, my friend. That's all I can say."

"I told you, she's the one. If I can't win her over, maybe I'll sell the house to you and Becky. Don't tell me you don't want a bunch of kids. I know how much you hate being an only child."

"Yeah, well, we haven't exactly talked about that subject yet. We're young. No need to rush."

"I'm not rushing. I'm planning. There's a difference."

"Whatever. Sounds like you're putting the cart before the horse to me, but what do I know?"

"You know nothing. I thought we established that years ago," Scott teased. Ford was the brother he'd never had growing up, and they behaved like siblings more often than not. Settling in his friend's hometown felt right. "I need you to do me a favor."

"Oh no. Please don't ask me to keep all this from Becky."

"Well, that, too, but I was hoping I could convince you not to invite my parents to your wedding."

"She's going to meet your parents sometime."

"You've met them. Roseanne's blood isn't blue enough for them. They aren't going to approve of her, and I don't want them scaring her off."

Ford shrugged. "I'll see what I can do. It might be too late, though. One of the first things Roseanne did was ask for a guest list so she could send it to someone to hand address all the envelopes."

"Shit." Scott chugged the rest of his beer. "Why do these things have to be planned so far in advance?"

"Hell if I know. I didn't see anything wrong with our Vegas wedding."

"It was legal, so what's the big deal?"

"Asking the wrong person. I'm just following my dad's advice."

"What advice is that?"

"Happy wife, happy life."

Scott nodded. "Sound advice if I ever heard any."

CHAPTER SEVEN

Knowing the source of her illness made it worse, not better. With the help of her best friend, Roseanne made an appointment with a doctor in Prairieview. She came away from the first visit elated and stunned at the enormity of what she was doing. Having been an only child, she'd dreamed of having a big family, but as the years had gone by and no eligible candidates for husband and father had come along, she'd shoved the dream to the back of her mind and focused on living life as it came.

This is my life now, she thought, caressing her still-flat belly with one hand as she steered the car with the other.

There was no going back. What was done was done, and she wouldn't change a thing. The kid was probably doomed to being an only child, too, but Roseanne vowed she would do the best she could to raise a happy and healthy child. He or she would have all the love she could give, and then some. She briefly thought about telling her parents, but decided against telling them—for now. They'd just see this as another screw-up on her part and demand she hold the baby's father up for every cent she could. Her dad would probably offer to file the lawsuit for her.

She didn't want Scott's money and doubted he'd want anything to do with the child. She would tell him about the baby, but when she was good and ready.

Determined not to take money from Scott, she considered her options. The bed-and-breakfast was doing okay these days, but the earning potential there was finite. Which meant she needed to pursue the cookbook idea. Eventually, she'd need another place to live, too. She could easily keep an infant in her room at

The Yellow Rose, but once the child was old enough to sleep in a real bed, she'd have a problem. Converting a guest room to a private room for her kid would reduce the room inventory by one, ensuring the inn would fail. The numbers barely worked as it was. Of course, if she moved out, there would be yet another room to rent, which would offset the cost of renting another house for her and the baby. That also meant there wouldn't be a caretaker on premises. That wouldn't do. Maybe she could convert the garage to an apartment for herself and her child. She mentally calculated the square footage, determined it could work, but the idea met a brick wall. Where would she find the funds for the conversion?

Thinking about all the challenges ahead for her as a single parent made her head hurt. She reached the exit for Butte Plains and smiled at the makeshift nameplate someone had recently added to the exit sign, declaring her hometown to be Butt Plug instead of Butte Plains. The sign alterations had started appearing shortly after Ford and Becky put the town on the map as the home of the now-famous sex toy that had saved Adams Manufacturing from bankruptcy and brought the town back from the edge of extinction. The department of transportation removed the sign alternations regularly, but they always came back. Photos of the signs had gone viral on the internet, which had helped spread the word about the new adult toy and increase sales.

Thinking about Ford and Becky reminded her she needed to stop by the florist and go over the details for the wedding she would be hosting in a couple of months. She did a mental calculation based on what the doctor had told her and concluded she wouldn't be showing then. That was a good thing, as the father of her baby would be the best man to her maid of honor status. If she was showing, there'd be no way to avoid telling him about the child.

Roseanne pulled into a parking spot in front of the floral shop on the edge of downtown. Encouraged by the upswing in the economy, the owners, who had closed their doors a few years ago, had recently reopened. From the number of cars in the lot, business was good. She grabbed the notebook she was never without and entered the store.

"Roseanne!"

"Hello, Mrs. Bullard. I brought my notes on the wedding I spoke to you about. Do you have time to go over them?"

"I'll make time. Let me finish this order, and I'll be right with you."

"No problem. I think I'll wait outside. Just give me a whistle when you're ready." Roseanne had inherited her grandmother's love of flowers, but in the enclosed space the fragrant blooms turned her stomach. Settled on the wooden bench out front, she took a deep breath and willed the nausea to go away. It didn't take much these days to make her gut uneasy, and strong smells were often the culprit. Feeling better, she opened her notebook and refreshed her memory. Becky hadn't been specific regarding her floral choices, but knowing her friend the way she did, pink was a must. She jotted down a few things that popped into her head regarding the arrangements. When it looked like Mrs. Bullard was going to be a while longer, Roseanne flipped to the new section she'd started at the doctor's office and began a new list. In a few short minutes, she had filled an entire page with things she would need for the baby.

Wow. Who would have thought? Overwhelmed with the task ahead of her, she didn't hear the florist approach. "Oh! I'm sorry. I guess I was woolgathering."

"Not a problem. I'm sorry to have kept you waiting."

With her index finger wedged between the pages, she held the notebook up. "As you can see, I kept busy."

"I brought mine, too," the older woman said, indicating the thick binder she held against her chest. "It's nice out here today. Would you mind if we sat here to go over the plans?"

"Not at all. Please, join me." Roseanne scooted over to make room for the floral merchant. They talked for nearly an hour, as neither one wanted to leave anything to chance.

When they were through, Mrs. Bullard closed her binder and sighed. "This is going to be a lovely wedding. I'm so happy for Ford and Becky. They make a beautiful couple."

"Yes, they do, and, thanks to you, their wedding is going to be stunning."

"I appreciate the chance to be a part of their day, and if I might say so, I hope to be a part of yours sometime soon, too."

Roseanne's stomach did a backflip. "Don't hold your breath, Mrs. Bullard."

"I don't know. Lots of new people are moving into town. You never know when the right one will suddenly appear."

"You're a true romantic." Uneasy with the turn of the conversation, Roseanne stood. Mrs. Bullard did the same. For the first time since she'd realized she was pregnant, she wondered what the people in town would think. She certainly wouldn't be the first unwed mother in Butte Plains, but she couldn't recall one who had maintained her reputation in the community. Well, she wasn't going to force Scott to marry her just so people wouldn't talk. This was the twenty-first century, after all.

"It never hurts to look through rose-colored glasses, dear."

"Whatever." Roseanne laughed and forced a smile to her lips. "I've got to be going. Call me if you have any questions; otherwise, we're good to go, right?"

"Right. Scoot on along. I've got it under control."

Well, that makes one of us. "Thanks, Mrs. Bullard. Oh, and I'll have Kay call you to let you know how many arrangements we'll need for the rooms next week." Ever since the florist had reopened, Roseanne had been ordering small arrangements for the rented rooms and the front hallway. She preferred to use blooms from her own garden, but the plants hadn't been able to keep up with the demand. It was a nice problem to have. She hoped she'd be able to continue purchasing the fresh flowers, but if things got real tight with the new baby, the flower arrangements would be one of the first things she'd cut from the budget. Artificial flowers and some essential oils in a diffuser would be less expensive over time.

"I'll order in more yellow roses, just in case."

"Thanks!" Roseanne ducked into the safety of her car and cranked the engine. *Whew!* She put the car in gear and exited the lot. Suddenly hungry and tired, she couldn't wait to get home and be alone for a few minutes. Maybe get in a nap. Her cell phone rang. She pulled over and fished the device out of her purse. There wasn't any money in the budget for a newfangled car with Bluetooth and likely would never be now. "Hi, Kay, what's up?"

"Ms. Meadows, I'm sorry to bother you, but there are some people here from the rental company. They say the tent you ordered isn't going to fit on the lawn. Something about fire clearances. Can you come talk to them?"

Roseanne cupped her forehead between the thumb and middle finger of her free hand and resisted the urge to cry. Breaking down now wouldn't fix anything. "I'm almost home, Kay. Give them some sweet tea and cookies and tell them I'll be along in a few minutes."

"Will do. If I knew what to tell them, I'd save you the trouble."

"No worries. I'm sure it can all be sorted out in a matter of minutes."

"Okay. Drive safe."

Roseanne disconnected and clenched the phone in her fist. She closed her eyes and took a minute to find her center before pulling back onto the road. One more hurdle today then she'd get that nap. One block away from the B&B, she stopped in the middle of the road and stared at the work taking place on the old Victorian she'd admired and worried about for so long. Once a grand lady much like her grandmother's house, only bigger, the place had been vacant for decades and was little more than a ruin. She'd been concerned someone would come in and buy it just for the lot. Judging from the giant equipment on the lawn, that's exactly what had happened.

"Hey! Lady!" A guy wearing a hard hat and dusty work clothes yelled at her from the sidewalk.

Roseanne rolled her window down. "What?"

"You need to move. We've got a dumpster coming in, and you're blocking the way." He pointed at something behind her. She glanced in the rearview mirror and saw the giant truck with the big trash dumpster about a foot off her bumper.

"Okay. I'm going." She rolled the window up and crept down the street. "But I'll be back," she muttered. As soon as she got rid of the tent people, she'd return to the construction site and find out what was going on. If it wasn't too late, maybe the historical society could step in and save the structure. Taking one last look at the place in her mirror, she had the sinking feeling it was too late.

The tent issue proved to be easily solved. There had been a misunderstanding about where, exactly, she wanted them to put it. Once that was corrected, the problem went away. Roseanne took the opportunity to review the placement of the stage, dance floor, and tables with them. Better to find out now if there was a problem than to deal with it at the last minute. Assured everything was squared away with the rental company, Roseanne made her way to the back door and let herself into the kitchen. She grabbed a glass of sweet tea before heading upstairs to her room on the third floor. Winded when she finally collapsed on her bed, she wondered how she would manage the climb when she could no longer see her feet.

Ugh. Something else to worry about! She closed her eyes and willed the tension from her body. A few minutes…then she'd get up.

Beep. Beep. Beep.

Roseanne popped one eye open. The annoying sound continued, so she sat up, looking around for the source. Eventually, she wandered over and opened the window. The sound grew louder, followed by a loud crash.

"The house!" She'd forgotten all about the construction crew around the corner.

She flew down the stairs, grabbed a

water bottle from the fridge, and cut through the backyard to the alley that ran behind her house. The old Victorian looked worse from this angle than it did from the front, and that was saying something. Someone had chopped down the overgrown foliage, creating a path around to the front. Roseanne followed it, coming to an abrupt halt when she came face-to-face with a skid loader.

She placed a hand on her chest to still her wildly beating heart.

"Better get out of the way, lady."

"No. I'm not budging until I speak to whoever is in charge."

"What is this? Some kind of intervention? We have permits."

"I want to see those permits." Everyone at City Hall knew better than to issue a demolition permit for a century-old home without consulting the Historical Society first. She fisted her hands on her hips and tilted her chin up. "Who's in charge here?"

"Hold on." He grabbed a walkie-talkie from a pocket next to the seat and spoke into it. "Randy? We've got a problem here. Can you come take care of it?"

The radio squawked then a voice said, "I'm kind of busy here. Can't you take care of it?"

"No can do, boss. Lady says she wants the man in charge." The equipment operator winked at Roseanne.

"What lady?" the voice asked.

"He wants to know who you are."

"I heard him," Roseanne said. "Tell him I'm from the Historical Society."

He raised one eyebrow and lifted the walkie-talkie. "She's from the Historical Society." Distain dripped from the words.

"On my way."

CHAPTER EIGHT

Roseanne smirked. It was amazing what those few words could accomplish. If there was one thing construction people hated, it was someone with the power to shut them down.

The machine in front of her cut off, and the operator climbed out. "Taking a break," he said.

With no one to intimidate, Roseanne relaxed her shoulders and took a moment to look around. Edging past the machinery, she could see not one, but two giant trash receptacles parked on the front lawn. While she watched, a couple of boards flew out a front window, landing with a thud in the nearest bin. If she was going to save the house, she'd have to work fast. They were already tearing it apart, one board at a time.

The front door opened, and a tall, slender man wearing a hard hat and carrying a clipboard took the rickety steps to the yard at a brisk clip. He wore a dark-green button-down shirt, tan slacks, and tasseled loafers. Stopping to speak with a guy Roseanne recognized as the man from the skid loader, he glanced her way. He clapped the other man on the shoulder, said something she couldn't hear, but assumed was reassuring. Then he focused on her, and, with two trash Dumpsters and an expanse of unkempt lawn between them, she felt his gaze all the way down to her toes.

He approached slowly, as if he had all the time in the world. Roseanne took a deep breath and held her ground. Lord, he was good-looking! Short-cropped sandy hair peeked from beneath the hard hat which shaded deep-blue eyes. Scruff a shade darker than his hair emphasized the strong line of his jaw. He walked with a rolling gate that spoke of athleticism.

The Yankee Billionaire's Bride

When he spoke, his voice seemed to come from the depths of a very deep well and rolled over her like water from a hot spring. "Hello. I'm Randy Tucker." He pointed to the logo embroidered on the left side of his shirt, which she could now see was a very nice fabric that had probably cost a pretty penny. "Tucker Construction. What can I do for you, Ms...?"

She shook off her attraction to the man. Handsome or not, he was the enemy. "Meadows. Roseanne Meadows. I'm a member of the Butte Plains Historical Society. Do you have a permit to demolish this house?"

"No, we do not have a permit to demolish the house."

"Then I insist you stop, at once."

A dimple appeared in his right cheek. If she'd been in the market for a man, his smile would have overridden her concerns about him tearing down the house. But she wasn't in the market for a man—she'd had one too many of those already. "No can do, Ms. Meadows. We have a schedule to keep."

"I don't give a tinker's damn about your schedule. You will shut down now, or I'll call the police and have them shut you down."

"That won't be necessary, ma'am." He leafed through the papers on his clipboard, found the one he wanted, and released it from the clamp. "We have all the permission we need."

Roseanne snatched the official-looking document out of his hand. "This is a permit—"

"To restore the structure. Yes, ma'am. It might look like we're tearing the place down, but rest assured, we'll replace everything we tear out. We specialize in restoring historic homes and buildings." He reached into his breast pocket, withdrew a card, and handed it over, taking the permit from her at the same time. "Feel free to check out our website."

"Who?" She didn't know what to say. Someone was actually restoring the place? That had to cost a fortune. "Who are you working for?"

"Outfit called BP Investments. We've been hired to restore several structures in town. If you have any questions, you'd best ask them."

She'd never heard of the company. "Do you have an address or phone number for them?"

"Their office is in Dallas, I think. I can give you the number for my contact there."

"Please." She handed him back his card. He consulted his phone, turned his business card over, and wrote on the back.

"Guy's name is Riley Ashworth." He returned the card to her. "Nice fella."

Roseanne glanced at the neat handwriting. The name and number weren't at all familiar. "You said you were hired to renovate other properties in Butte Plains?"

"As soon as we get the deconstruction done on this one, we'll start on the others. A whole block of abandoned businesses on Main Street."

"Is the Cotton Exchange one of them?" She'd admired the structure since she was a kid. Built in 1861, it had been home to many things after the first owners moved out early in the twentieth century.

"You know the place?"

Roseanne nodded. "Everyone at the Historical Society does. You'll need approval from us to remove any of the details from the façade."

"Riley is supposed to be working on that, though the plans I've seen call for restoring the façade to its original condition, as well as retaining most of the interior. Anything that can't be saved will be replaced with new materials as close to the original as possible. When we're done, you won't be able to tell what's new and what's not."

"I hope you're as good as you think you are."

The moment the words left her mouth, she wished she could yank them back. The man standing before her smiled, revealing a matching dimple on his other cheek.

"I'm good, Ms. Meadows. Real good. You'll see." He tucked his clipboard next to his hip. "Hey, since you're here, I wonder if you can tell me anything about that yellow Victorian around the corner."

He pointed unnecessarily. The Yellow Rose was the only yellow Victorian in the entire town. "I know it. Why?"

"The owner of this property pointed it out as a possible source for inspiration on this renovation. Said the houses were built by the same contractor back in the day. It looks in good shape. Whoever did the restoration on it did a good job."

Roseanne bristled. "The Yellow Rose is mine. It was my grandmother's home, and what you see is original."

"Really? That's even better. What about the inside?"

"A few renovations have been done over the years, and I made some concessions in order to turn it into a bed-and-breakfast, but nothing that would compromise the integrity of the structure." She could see his interest growing as she spoke. Maybe he did have an appreciation for old buildings.

"I'd love to see inside, maybe take a few photos of the moldings and other details? Would that be okay?"

Roseanne nodded. "I suppose, if it

would help you restore this one."

"It would. Thank you. There's not much left to go on with this one. When would be a good time to come over?"

She thought about her crazy schedule for a second. "I don't know. I'm in the middle of planning a big event right now, but I suppose I could spare a few minutes. Maybe tomorrow afternoon around one? We'll be in between guests, and the rooms should be turned."

"It's a date, then. Now, unless you have something else to discuss, I need to get my men back to work."

"No. I'm good."

"I'm sure you are. Good day, Ms. Meadows."

She admired his firm butt as he walked away.

When he reached the steps, he let out a shrill whistle then yelled, "Everybody back to work."

An unholy racket began inside the house. Behind her, the skid loader started up again.

Roseanne made her way to the sidewalk, where she turned back and looked at the dilapidated structure with fresh eyes. She fingered the card Randy Tucker had given her. Lots of new people had come into town in the last few months, buying up real estate, hoping to make a profit on it.

"Probably some oil-rich corporation out of Dallas," she muttered.

At least they were restoring and not tearing down. She made a mental note to ask around, see if anyone knew what their endgame was.

CHAPTER NINE

The next day, promptly at one o'clock, the bell above the front door jingled. Roseanne stood and smoothed out the wrinkles in her skirt. She'd gone through several dress selections this morning before choosing this one—a summer-weight sleeveless cotton shift that fit her curves but was simple enough to retain a casual look. She had on strappy sandals with a low heel and she'd pulled her shoulder-length hair into a high ponytail. Daring the day's heat to do its worst, she'd applied a light layer of makeup. She told herself she was doing it to lift her spirits, not because Randy Tucker was coming to see the house. Besides, he was only interested in her house, and she had no business noticing his hunkiness anyway.

"Anyone home?"

His deep baritone sent a shiver down her spine. Must be the hormone cocktail her doctor had warned her about. Satisfied she looked as good as she was going to get, she called out, "Coming!" *Great. Great choice of words.*

She shook her head at her own stupidity then stepped into the hall. Randy Tucker stood there, his chin in the air as he examined the crown moldings in the entryway. His gaze traveled down, landing on her. His eyes widened. A smile brought out his dimples.

"Hello, again."

Roseanne smiled. After feeling like shit for the last few weeks, his admiring gaze lifted her spirits. "Welcome to The Yellow Rose." Maybe if she was nice to him, he might give her a good price on converting the garage to an apartment. If she could find a way to pay for the renovation.

"Thank you. This place is amazing."

His gaze returned to the hand-carved woodwork. "All this is original?"

She ran her hand over the ornate newel post. "It is. The kitchen is the only room on the main floor that has been renovated. Everything else you see is just as it was the day my grandparents moved in."

"They were the original owners?"

"Yep. My grandfather passed when I was about six, I think. My grandmother lived here until she passed ten years ago. The house was vacant for two years, until I finished college and moved back. It's been a bed-and-breakfast for the last six years."

He pulled out his cell phone. "Mind if I take some pictures?"

"Not at all." She turned on the ancient chandelier so he'd have better light.

"That's original, too?"

"Yep. I had the electrical inspected. At some point, my grandmother had the place rewired, and the plumbing upgraded to meet modern standards. However, the windows and doors are original. She didn't go so far as to modernize the charm out of the place."

"Your grandmother was a smart woman."

"Would you put that on a plaque? I'm sure my guests will appreciate it when they can't keep warm in the winter or cool in the summer."

"There are ways to alleviate some of the drafts. I'll know more once I see the drafty windows in question."

"I doubt I could afford whatever solutions you come up with. I'm barely hanging on as it is."

He snapped several pictures, including one of the window moldings in the front parlor. "If the energy savings were enough, it would be worth the investment."

"Investment. That's the key word. It supposes one has money to invest, which I don't."

He shrugged. "Maybe sometime in the future, then." He roamed the public rooms, taking photo after photo, both close-up and from a wide angle. When he was done, he asked, "Can I see the kitchen? You said it has been remodeled?"

"Sure. Come on." She led the way into what she considered her haven. Her small staff had completed their work for the day and left, except for Kay who would be back later to check in the guests arriving today. A plate of muffins leftover from breakfast sat in the center of the large, marble-topped island.

Randy let out a low whistle. "Wow. This is amazing."

"The cabinets are original, except for the island. My grandmother had that built about twenty years ago. I had all the old countertops replaced with marble, and put in a new sink and appliances to meet code for a commercial kitchen."

"You and your grandmother did a great job. I'm sure the builder would have used these materials if they'd been available to him." He ran his hand appreciatively over the cold stone counter. "Pictures?"

"Sure. Go ahead." She stood back as he roamed the room, clicking away. She'd had a few guests who loved old houses and wanted to see everything, and learn the history of the place, but none had ever paid such close attention to the details. Randy photographed everything, down to the hinges on the cabinet doors and the shelving in the pantry.

"I can't tell you how helpful this is. My carpenters and designers are going to want to see this place. The photos will help, but nothing beats seeing it in person."

"They're welcome anytime. Would you like to see the guest rooms?"

"Lead the way, pretty lady. I'll look at anything you want to show me."

Roseanne blushed.

He noticed and quickly amended his statement. "Sorry. I meant, I'll look at any part of the *house* you want to show me."

Roseanne's laugh sounded nervous even to herself. This was ridiculous. She was acting like a hormonal teenager when she had zero interest in doing anything with the man. If she were being honest with herself, she wished she was having this conversation with Scott Ramsey. Despite his lack of interest in her, she still loved him, and, thanks to the child she carried, he'd always be a part of her life. She'd made up her mind to tell him after Ford and Becky's wedding. She planned to make it perfectly clear she wanted nothing from him, but hoped he'd at least want to be a part-time parent. If he didn't, well, fuck him. They'd do just fine without him.

"I know what you meant. Come on." He followed her up the back staircase to the second floor. "There are three bedrooms on this level, and one on the third floor." She pointed out the bathroom that two of the rooms shared, mentioning that the Senator's Suite had its own bathroom. Naturally, he wanted to see it all.

"If you don't mind, I'll leave you to look around. I have some phone calls I need to make." There seemed to be no end to the details regarding the upcoming wedding. She still needed to find someone to provide the audio-visual equipment for both the ceremony and the reception. "I'll unlock the other rooms for you before I go."

"That's fine. I don't want to take up all your time. Honestly? I could spend days here, looking at everything, but I'll leave that to my crew. I just need to get enough photos to get them started."

"I'll be in my office." She started to leave. "Oh. Do you need to see the third floor? There's only one room with a small bathroom. The rest is attic space."

"I wouldn't mind seeing the attic. I suspect your room is much like the ones down here?"

"It's directly above us, and nearly identical to this suite."

"Then I'll settle for seeing the attic. Is it open?"

"Never saw a need to lock it. Have fun exploring." She made her way downstairs to her office. She'd heard the phone ring several times since Mr. Tucker had arrived. There were several messages, one about the audio/visual equipment and two others were customers inquiring about available rooms. She returned those first because, without customers, she'd have to close her doors. When she finally got off the phone, having successfully negotiated a price for the delivery, setup, and maintenance of the equipment she needed, she sat back in her chair and closed her eyes.

"You look peaceful sitting there."

Roseanne nearly jumped out of her skin at the sound of the masculine voice so close by. "Oh!"

Randy Tucker leaned casually in the doorway to her office. The smile on his face said he wasn't at all sorry about scaring the bejeezus out of her.

"I'd forgotten you were here."

"Good thing I'm not a serial killer, then."

She allowed herself a smile. "I suppose so. Did you see enough?"

"Not nearly enough," he said, his gaze raking over the modest neckline of her dress. "But enough for now. Mind if I bring some people over in a couple of days?"

"If you could call first, that would be good. I don't want to inconvenience my guests."

"Not a problem." He held up one of the colorful brochures she'd had printed to advertise the inn locally. She kept a few on the table in the foyer for her guests to take with them. "Can I reach you at the number listed here?"

Roseanne held her hand out. "Here. Let me give you my private number." After scribbling her cell phone number on the brochure, she handed it to him. "This time of day is usually good."

"I heard you on the phone. You host special events?"

"This is my first—a wedding for my best friend. I want everything to be perfect."

"I'm sure it will be. Who wouldn't want to get married in a place like this?"

"The ceremony will be in the garden. We're putting a giant tent on the front lawn for the reception. We'll have a catered meal, dancing, and live entertainment. It's going to be quite a shindig."

"Sounds like it. I saw the garden from the upstairs window. Mind if I take a closer look? My client wants something similar—thus the skid loader you met yesterday. We need access to the rear of the house, so I told them we'd clear the overgrown brush out of the way so the landscapers could get a better look."

"Gardens like mine don't spring up overnight. My grandmother planted most of it when she first moved in. It's taken decades of hard work to get it the way it is."

"May I see it?"

"Sure. I could use a break and some fresh air." She led the way through the kitchen and out the back door. Pausing on the wide porch, she spread her arms out. "This is it."

"Wow." He took the steps slowly, his gaze sweeping from side to side as he took it all in. "You tend to this yourself?"

"Yep. I learned from my grandmother. She was a much better gardener than I ever will be."

"You're doing a great job. No wonder your friend wants to have her wedding here. Have you thought about renting it out for weddings?"

"Up until recently, there hasn't been much call for social events in Butte Plains, but now that the town is growing again, I might. We'll see how this one goes. There's a lot involved." And, with a baby to take care of, her time was going to be limited. Once this one was done, she'd have contacts for the rentals, so maybe she could hire someone to coordinate with the bride and groom. All she'd have to do was collect the money and pay the bills.

"The town is growing by leaps and bounds. I'd think a venue like this could be successful. You should give it some thought."

"I will. Thanks." They strolled the gravel pathways in silence while he took photos. Roseanne wiped a bead of sweat from her forehead.

"I'd better get back. I'm supposed to meet with my designer and head carpenter later. I can't wait to show them these pictures." Roseanne pointed out the shortcut she'd used the other day then watched as he found his way to the construction site. Her grandmother would be so proud to know her home and gardens were being used as inspiration to save another grand old home.

While she'd been out back, Kay had come in through the front. They met up in the kitchen. "Is it that time already?" Roseanne asked.

"It will be soon. Our first guest for the night should be here soon. I just wanted to check the rooms out one more time, make sure everything is shipshape."

"That's a good idea." She told her assistant about letting Mr. Tucker photograph the rooms. "I doubt he moved anything, but just in case."

"Thanks for letting me know. I'll be sure to look for anything out of place on my mini-tour." She folded a dish rag and hung it neatly over the edge of the sink. "If he brings the others at an inconvenient time for you, I'd be happy to show them around. I think it's wonderful that The Yellow Rose will be a part of restoring that house to its former glory."

"Me, too. I don't know who bought the place, but they can't be all bad if they're willing to pay what it must cost to restore the old girl to her former glory."

Kay shook her head. "That must cost a fortune. Just look at what a tract house costs these days."

"I know. It's crazy what people pay for cookie-cutter construction. Give me an old house, drafts and all any day."

"I'm with you. My place isn't anywhere as grand as yours, but it's a far cry from those ugly boxes they're building out near the freeway." She glanced at her watch. "Better go check the rooms. I'll listen for the bell, so don't you worry. I've got this under control."

The older woman hurried off. Roseanne poured herself a glass of sweet tea from the pitcher in the refrigerator, grabbed a muffin from the plate in the center of the kitchen island, and headed to her office. A few more details then she'd call it a day.

CHAPTER TEN

"You were able to tour The Yellow Rose?" Scott had hoped the contractor would take his advice and visit the bed-and-breakfast for inspiration. Roseanne loved her grandmother's home, and nothing short of a dwelling equally as spectacular would ever convince her to leave it. That's why he'd hired Tucker Construction. They had a reputation as the best restoration specialist in Texas.

"The owner herself gave me the tour. Thanks for pointing me in the right direction. I took a zillion pictures. I thought my designer was going to swoon, and my carpenter almost had a heart attack at the thought of having to recreate some of those details."

"If he's not up to the task, find someone who is. Money is no object."

"You sure about that? This is going to cost a fortune. All that woodwork has to be handcrafted. Can't pick that stuff off the shelves these days."

"I'm sure. Whatever it takes. Just send me the bill."

"I will, don't worry. And I'm sure my carpenter is up to the task. His concern is the timeline. He doesn't want to rush."

"I'm anxious to see the place finished, but tell him to take as long as he needs to do it right. And since money is no object, if he knows someone skilled enough to help him, hire him."

"Got it. I'll tell him." He went on about the progress being made, throwing out questions Scott answered or jotted down to think about. Since he planned to live there the rest of his life with Roseanne and their brood of kids, he wanted to do it right.

"Anything else?"

"Just that if you want a garden to rival the one at the bed-and-breakfast, you better hire a damned good gardener and landscape architect."

"Done, and done," Scott said. "Anything else?"

"You still want me to keep your name out of it? Refer any questions to Riley?"

"Until you hear otherwise from me. You okay with that?"

"You're the boss. Talk to you soon." The line went dead.

Scott stared at the screensaver on his cell phone. He'd taken the photo of Roseanne in Las Vegas. It was their first night in the glittering city, and they had tickets to see Becky's younger brother, Colin, perform at one of the casinos on the strip. Roseanne had outshone all the lights along the fabled road in her simple, classic evening gown. He'd begged her to let him take the picture. Other than a few candid shots, it was the only other one he had of her. He kept it front and center so he could look at it anytime he wanted to—a reminder of his goal—to make her his forever. Even if it took forever.

He hated living a stealth life, but he

didn't have much choice. As long as Roseanne thought he had no ties to Butte Plains, she wasn't going to have anything to do with him. He couldn't blame her. Her life was here, and it was a good one. He'd never dream of asking her to give it up to move to a place where she didn't know a soul or have any ties with the community. It was much easier for him to pick up and move since he'd never really felt like he belonged in the world into which he'd been born. It was only right that he make a home for himself and the family he wanted in a place of his choosing. And he chose Butte Plains.

The town had grown on him. Ford said like a fungus, but Scott knew better. The town had history. It had character. It had opportunity and challenge. All those things drew him there, made him want to add his mark to the future of the town. In the weeks since he'd left The Yellow Rose, his secretary, Riley, had successfully moved their entire office from New York to Dallas. The two of them had set up a corporation to buy and restore real estate in and around Butte

Plains, keeping Scott's name out of the transactions. He wanted to make his mark in the town, but didn't necessarily want the recognition that normally came along with dropping boatloads of cash in a small space. He'd rather see the longtime residents take pride in their hometown and rise to the occasion. He knew they would. The anonymous donation he'd made to the parks department had brought out a lot of enthusiastic people to clean up the town square in order for the city crews to come in and make the repairs necessary to make the place inhabitable again.

Dozens of folks had carried trash bags and sticks sharpened on the end to pick up litter. More had gathered fallen limbs and piled them for the landscapers to push through the chipper. Others had helped scrape peeling paint off the gazebo so it could be repainted. There were new trash receptacles on every corner downtown. Parking spaces had been restriped and light poles repaired. Planters had been purchased and hung from light standards. Newly washed windows sparkled in the sun. Tenants who hadn't done anything in years to enhance the curb appeal of their stores were painting and dressing windows with enticing displays.

Money could work wonders, but it was pride and hope that really made a difference. For the first time in his life, he felt that he'd been born wealthy for a reason.

~ ~ ~

"Did you get it?" Roseanne waved her assistant over to the side porch where she'd taken root while the workers lifted the heavy tent roof into place.

At Becky's request, she'd blocked out all the rooms in the B&B for wedding guests, but her friend had been crazy busy at work and had failed to give her a list of names to go with the bookings. Twenty-four hours away from the I do's and she still didn't have a list, so she'd sent Kay over to Adams Manufacturing to see if she could get it from Becky's secretary while Roseanne stayed behind to supervise the setting up of the tent in the front yard.

"Got it right here." Kay brandished a piece of yellow, lined paper as she approached. "How's the tent going?"

"It's getting there. I thought we were going to have to relocate the water line running from the street to the house, but they found another way to anchor the post in question." That snafu had almost sent her into a fit of tears. Lesser things certainly had in the last few weeks—like the tray of cookies she'd burned while looking at cribs online. She'd cried for an hour over the mess. Thank goodness the experienced workers had found a better way to secure the pole and moved on. Otherwise, she might have cried for a week. Absolutely nothing could go wrong with Becky's wedding. She'd made that vow to herself, and she planned on keeping it. She held her hand out. "Here. Let me see that."

It was a short list. They only had the three rooms, after all. She recognized the first one—a cousin to Ford's mother. The woman had stayed at the inn before and was easy to please. The second one would be a bit of a problem if anyone found out he was there. Becky's brother, Colin, had quite the following among teenage and young adult women. The last names on the list rocked Roseanne back against the porch railing. "Oh, no. No. This can't be right."

"What? Is there a problem? Are you okay?" Kay steered Roseanne to one of the rocking chairs lined up along the porch and helped her sit.

"Did you speak to Becky, or did her secretary give this to you?"

"I talked to Becky. As soon as I told the secretary why I was there, she showed me into Ms. Parker's office. She pulled this out of her desk drawer and handed it to me herself."

No wonder her friend hadn't given her the list until today. Becky had deliberately waited until it was too late to make changes. Besides, where else would she put up Scott's parents, June and Gerald Ramsey? The new cut-rate motel on the interstate certainly wouldn't do, and Ford's familial home was filled with Adams relatives and family friends. That left one place in town. Her place. *Damn you, Becky Jean Parker-Adams.* Roseanne swiped at the damp line streaking down her cheek.

"Is everything okay? Do you want me to call Ms. Parker?"

"No." She sniffed and straightened her spine. Tears would only smudge the writing, not make the problem go away. She sniffed and blinked a few times to clear her vision. "Nothing to be worried about." She handed the list back. "Put the Ramsey's in the Senator's Suite. Mrs. Ellis likes the pink room on the side of the house. I'm sure Colin won't mind taking the blue room that overlooks the front yard."

"You sure you're fine?" Kay seemed reluctant to leave her, so Roseanne stood and forced a smile for her assistant.

"I'm fine. Everything is fine. Tent is almost up. Our guests are squared away. Mr. McKenna delivered the champagne while you were gone. I didn't know Becky had ordered beer, but there's a bunch of that, too, along with liquor for the bars that will be set up in the tent."

"I hope there's room in the cooler everything."

"If not, can we find some picnic coolers? I'm sure Mr. McKenna will deliver some bags of ice if we need them."

"Good idea. I'll go down to the cellar and eyeball the situation. Don't worry about a thing. If we need more space, I know some people to call."

"You're a godsend, Kay. What would I do without you?"

"Pishposh. What nonsense." She waved away her employer's concern. "You know I'm not going anywhere— except to the cellar."

Soon, the tent was up. Roseanne went over the placement of the stage, dance floor, tables, and bars with the crew before going inside. Out of necessity, she'd put the fact that Scott's parents were going to be staying under her roof for the next few days out of her mind, but the minute she sat down, her concerns came roaring back. Did Scott know? Surely he'd offered them a room in the gatehouse he was staying in on the

Adams estate. Maybe he didn't know they were attending the wedding. She dismissed that idea as soon as she thought it. Scott and the groom were thick as thieves. Why else would Ford invite Scott's parents to his wedding?

"Nothing I can do about it now," she muttered to herself. She'd look like an ungracious ogre if she asked Becky to find another place for them to stay. This new wrinkle put her in an awkward position. She'd planned on telling Scott about the baby after the wedding, but with his parents under her roof, she couldn't see doing so. She'd come off as the world's biggest gold digger. She could see it now. "Welcome to The Yellow Rose, and oh, by the way…I'm pregnant with your first grandchild."

Yeah, that would go over well. Ramsey lawyers would descend on her like a swarm of locusts, demanding tests and custody contracts. A sudden pain stabbed at her brain, like she'd drunk an ice-cold beverage too fast. Lord, she'd never thought about Scott and his family wanting custody of her child. She couldn't afford lawyers to fight the kind of battle they could wage. What judge wouldn't see they could provide everything she couldn't? She'd lose custody for sure.

I can't tell them. Not now, at least. Not until I have a lawyer and know more about my rights. She'd take the name of the baby's father to her grave before she'd let a bunch of rich strangers take her child away from her.

She reached for the small directory she kept with names and numbers of business contacts. Her hands shook as she thumbed through the pages until she found the listing she had in mind. Hank was an old friend who had grown up in Butte Plains and now had a law office in Dallas. He'd handled the probate of her grandmother's estate years ago. With a little luck, he'd still consider her a client, as well as a friend, and give her a good rate on advice.

Taking a deep breath, she dialed his number.

CHAPTER ELEVEN

Scott watched the Ramsey jet's wheels touch down on the runway. "Hot damn! Looked smooth as a baby's butt."

"Congratulations," Ford said. "Your new airstrip is officially christened."

"It took long enough. All those permits to reopen the place, not to mention replacing the outdated runway and getting the tower recertified. I was beginning to think it wouldn't ever happen."

"Well, it has, and it's fitting that your parents were the first ones to land here."

Scott nodded. "Yeah. But don't expect them to be enthusiastic about it. They're here to change my mind about making this my permanent home." He glanced around the small but well-appointed building that functioned as the office, waiting area, and control tower. The remodel had been expensive, most of the money going to the tower equipment. Right now, he couldn't justify the money he was spending to keep a full-time air traffic controller on duty, but he hoped traffic would pick up once people learned the airstrip was back in operation and better than ever.

"Here they come." Ford pointed out the window. A golf cart driven by one of his employees headed their way. His father rode in the front next to the driver, his mother in the back. "There's still time. I could ask my mother to put them up at her house. The Yellow Rose isn't exactly a five-star resort."

"Granted, I wish that invitation to your wedding had never been sent, but since they're here, they might as well see what this town is all about. Besides, my dad grew up in a house almost identical to Roseanne's. He should feel right at home." Scott laughed at his own joke.

"If you say so."

Clearly, Ford wasn't convinced. Scott hated saddling Roseanne with the Ramseys, but he had little choice. He just hoped his parents brought their manners with them. If they didn't, and insulted Roseanne or her home, there might be pistols at dawn. If it came to that, he'd bet on Roseanne any day. His parents wouldn't stand a chance.

Scott pushed the wide, glass doors open. "Mom. Dad. Welcome to Butte Plains Airport."

The older couple's smiles were as plastic as their sunglasses.

"It's good to see you, son." Gerald Ramsey clapped Scott on the back. "Ford! Congratulations!"

"Thank you, sir." Ford and the elder Ramsey shook hands.

June Ramsey followed close on the heels of her husband, giving first her son then Ford a hug. Her gaze scanned the space that constituted the public spaces. "This is so nice, Scott. Look, Gerald." She pointed to a large painting hanging over an arrangement of black leather chairs.

"That's lovely."

"It's an original painting by a local artist," Scott said. "I bought several of his pieces for the building. The rest are down the hall and in the pilot's lounge."

"I'd love to see them. May I?" June asked.

"Sure. This way." Scott led them through the building, stopping so his mother could admire the artwork. This, at least, he knew wasn't fake. His mother had always had an interest in art. She'd spent a small fortune on the paintings that graced the walls of their Hamptons estate.

June paused in front of a landscape depicting a West Texas sunset. The colors were vibrant and the setting serene. "Makes you want to go there, doesn't it?"

"Nothing keeping us from doing that," Gerald said.

"We've never really explored Texas," she said. "Maybe we should."

"Let's get Ford married then we'll see. I'd love to have that painting or one like it."

"I don't know if I want to part with this one," Scott said, "but you can speak with the artist. I think he has more in that series. He'd probably part with one of them for the right price."

"Oh, I'm so excited," his mother said. "Who knew we'd find something like this in Texas?" You would have thought she'd just landed on Mars. Scott kept that thought to himself and showed them to the next room.

"There's a lot more to the state than most people know," Ford said. "Everything from wide-open spaces in the west to dense forest in the east, rolling hills and lakes in the central section, and some of the most beautiful beaches in the world along the Gulf Coast. You could spend a lifetime here and not see it all."

"Then we've got to at least hit the highlights, Gerald."

"I agree, June. Let's get settled in. We don't want to be late for the rehearsal dinner tonight. Gotta meet the filly who convinced Ford to settle down." He winked at his son's best friend.

"Becky is excited to meet you, too," Ford said. "Come on. Scott and I will drop you off at the bed-and-breakfast then we've got to run a couple of errands before the shindig tonight." They made their way out to the parking area where Scott's new Land Rover waited for them. Someone had already piled their luggage in the back.

"Scott said the wedding and reception will be on the lawn?" His mother peered over her designer lenses at Ford.

"That's right. The Yellow Rose has one of the most beautiful gardens in the county, maybe in all of Texas. The owner is also Becky's best friend, Roseanne Meadows. Her grandparents bought the house when they first married and put in the garden. Roseanne has done a great job of keeping it up since she inherited and turned the house into a bed-and-breakfast."

"It reminds me of Grandmother Ramsey's house," Scott said.

"Is it as drafty as my mother's home?" Gerald asked.

As he'd feared, they'd left the better

part of their manners in New York. Scott shrugged. "You always said those were ghosts, not drafts."

"That's what Granddad always told me. It was a crock of shit but kept me from complaining about how cold the place was."

"Well, as hot as it is this summer, you won't have to worry about drafts at The Yellow Rose," Scott said.

"Please tell me it's air-conditioned." Gerald pulled a handkerchief from his pocket and wiped imaginary sweat from his brow.

"Trust me, Dad. You're going to love it." Scott glanced in the rearview mirror at his dad, his expression warning the older man to hush.

Ford mouthed, "It's not too late," then turned to look out the windshield when Scott shook his head.

They pulled into the driveway of the inn a few minutes later. The giant tent on the front lawn kept them from seeing the front of the house, but the side view was almost as impressive.

"Oh my," June exclaimed. "I see what

you mean, Scott. This is so much like Grandmother Ramsey's house." She walked around to the wide steps leading to the front door.

"I stayed here the first few months I was in town," Scott said. "Wait until you see the woodwork. It's all hand carved." And worth a fortune, he now knew. The man he'd hired to replicate the moldings for the house around the corner was charging him an arm and a leg.

Ford bounded up the stairs and opened the front door. A bell jingled, alerting the staff.

"This is beautiful," June said, running her hand over the stained glass insert in the door, depicting a bouquet of yellow roses. "Is this original to the house?"

"Yes, it is." At the sound of the familiar woman's voice, Scott looked up. Roseanne stood in the entryway, looking tired but beautiful. She wore tan slacks and a sleeveless blouse in cream. Her hair was pulled up in a high ponytail, revealing tiny gold earrings and the slim column of her neck. When she extended her hand to his mother, he noticed her nails were painted a pale pink—probably to match the dress she would wear tomorrow as Becky's bridesmaid. "My grandmother said she wanted that window, and the only way she could get it was to buy the whole house. So, she convinced my grandfather to purchase it for her as a wedding present."

"That's so romantic," June said, taking Roseanne's hand. "I'm June Ramsey, and this is my husband, Gerald."

"Roseanne Meadows. Welcome to The Yellow Rose."

"I grew up in a house very much like this one," Gerald said. "Cold as a well digger's ass in the winter and hot as Hades in the summer."

"Then you know all about the quirks of an old house," Roseanne said. How she managed to keep her smile in place, he'd never know.

"You mean the creaking floors?"

"And the wavy glass in the windows," Roseanne added. "All the windows in the house are original, handmade glass. I thought about replacing them with modern, double-pane windows but decided the energy savings wasn't enough to sacrifice the historic detail."

"Humph."

"Gerald!" June scolded her husband.

"Let me show you to your room." Roseanne started up the stairs, leaving them to follow.

Scott caught Roseanne's gaze when she stopped and opened the door to the Senator's Suite. Had she purposely arranged for his parents to sleep in the same bed where he and Roseanne had made love countless times? Judging from the smirk on her face, yes, she'd done it on purpose.

He followed his folks into the room and hefted the two suitcases he'd carried onto the bed. Ford came in with two more. His parents thought packing light meant no dark-colored clothing.

"Is this all there is?" his father asked as he took one step into the bathroom, coming back out as if he expected the room to have miraculously expanded.

"You have a full bath, queen-sized bed, writing desk, and armoire. You'll find extra towels stacked in the armoire."

Roseanne recited her innkeeper's speech with mechanical precision.

He could almost see her calculating which object in the room would make the biggest dent in his father's head.

The paperweight. No sooner had he thought it than her gaze landed on the blown glass object sitting on the desk. She'd never in a million years actually bash him on the head, but he gave her kudos for thinking it. She wasn't going to take any guff off his parents, and that pleased him to no end.

"We'll be fine," his mother said, ushering them out in that way she had of being polite while still telling you to fuck off.

They went. The last one out, Scott paused. "Rehearsal is at six. No need for you to be there. Dinner will be in the dining room downstairs. See you then."

As soon as he and Ford were in the car, Scott said, "That went well."

"It went better than I expected."

Scott backed out of the driveway and pointed the SUV north. "First, tell me where we're going." Becky had made him swear to keep Ford on task today and tomorrow, and he was taking his duty seriously.

"Back to the airstrip. I chartered a private plane for Becky's brother."

"Where's he staying?"

"Same place as your parents."

"Oh, boy. That's going to be interesting."

"It's not as interesting as the reason you didn't invite Roseanne to your parents' party, so give."

Scott braked for a four-way stop. He let another car turn in front of him before proceeding through the intersection. "Let's just say I had my head stuck up my ass at the time. That's my only excuse."

"That's a valid excuse. Are you going to tell her about the house or the buildings you bought?"

"Not yet. As long as I'm living in your mother's gatehouse, I'm still a temporary resident. Once I've got my roots sunk deep, I'll tell her."

"So, you're going to stay even if she doesn't come around?"

"Yep. Everything I want is here. My

woman, my businesses, my best friend…and his wife. The great state of Texas is stuck with me. Is there a test I have to take to officially become a Texan?" He swung the car into the parking area at the airstrip. Other than the cars parked in the spaces reserved for employees, theirs was the only vehicle in the lot. He hoped that changed soon as others in the region learned the airstrip had reopened.

"It's called a driver's test. Pass that and you're official."

"I did that last week. Even registered to vote and bought a Lone Star Flag for the pole I'm putting up at the house."

"Sounds like you've got it covered, except for the accent. You might want to hire a speech therapist."

"Hey, I've picked up a few things. I can say y'all, over yonder, and thar as in, that thar is a plane." He pointed at the sky where a sleek jet angled toward the runway.

"That's a good start," Ford said as he reached for the door handle.

"Damn straight it is." Scott opened his

door.

PART TWO

"Even the rich are hungry for love, for being cared for, for being wanted, for having someone to call their own."
Mother Teresa

CHAPTER TWELVE

The big day had finally arrived. Roseanne had done all she could do, for the time being. Becky looked radiant in her designer gown, and Ford could have walked off the pages of GQ in his hand-tailored tux. From the bouquet of imported pink roses to the custom-made cake and sparkling champagne to be consumed later, no detail had been overlooked or compromised on. Roseanne had worked diligently to make the garden behind The Yellow Rose B&B a showplace fit to be the backdrop for the intimate gathering of friends and family, but as she listened to the groom pledge his eternal love, she let her gaze wander to the rose-covered trellis shading the happy couple. She'd used every gardening trick her grandmother had taught her, and her fingers had suffered, but the vines eventually submitted to her will, blooming beautifully to form the most romantic setting she could imagine.

Roseanne pressed the rumpled tissue to the corner of one eye then the other. Becky would never forgive her for having raccoon eyes in the post-ceremony photos, but damn, hearing her best friend pledge to love, honor, and cherish, even though it was only for show, had her fighting to keep the waterworks at bay. She'd been maid of honor at Ford and Becky's impromptu wedding in Las Vegas a few months ago, so it wasn't like she hadn't had time to get used to the idea, but that had been different. Yes, she'd been happy for the couple then, but in their haste to wed, they'd skimped on most everything that made a wedding special. Not so today. Though they could afford a much more elaborate affair, they'd gone for small and elegant instead.

Someone cleared their throat. Roseanne looked in the direction of the sound, and her gaze locked with her counterpart across the makeshift altar. The best man raised one eyebrow and cocked his head toward the bride and groom. Roseanne turned to see the officiant holding his prayer book out, his finger tapping the page.

Crap! She gave her best friend an apologetic smile and dropped the groom's ring in the center of the book. Across the way, the best man repeated the process with the bride's ring then captured Roseanne's gaze again. She looked away before the devilish smirk on Scott Ramsey's face lured her in. She'd fallen for it more times than she could count, but no more. There was much more at stake now. She couldn't afford the luxury of giving in to her desires. She'd done so before and look where it had gotten her—pregnant and single.

She returned the best man's gaze with a hard stare then focused all her attention on the smiling couple as they, without hesitation, professed their love for one another before God and as many people as could squeeze into the Victorian garden.

After a highly inappropriate kiss, Ford and Becky Adams faced the crowd then stepped off the small, raised platform. Amid cheers and applause, they made their exit. Steeling herself for Scott Ramsey's touch, Roseanne wrapped her fingers around the arm he offered, and, focusing on the retreating bride and groom, allowed the love of her life to escort her down the flower-strewn path to the bed-and-breakfast she called home.

"I should spank your ass for that," Scott said.

Despite her resolve to remain unaffected by him, his softly spoken comment hit its mark. Arousal tingled across her skin then made a beeline to the juncture of her thighs where it set up a primal drumbeat. Every step, every swish of pink chiffon against her skin exacerbated her condition until she thought she might expire from want of something she'd willfully given up. Once again, she questioned her decision to end their relationship. She missed their physical connection almost as much as she missed talking with him. He was smart, and funny, and a good storyteller. To say they were compatible in bed would be a gross understatement.

She caught a glimpse of his parents in the small crowd gathered to witness Ford and Becky's nuptials. Reality crashed down on her shoulders. Scott was more like them than he was like her. *And therein lies the problem.* Different worlds had collided and created a new universe.

The best she could hope for would be for Scott to go back to New York with his parents after the wedding. She'd wait a few months then call him and tell him about the baby. Just so he'd know, not because she wanted anything from him.

She risked a glance at her escort. From the moment she'd laid eyes on Scott Ramsey, she'd been a goner. Too handsome by far, he usually played his gorgeousness down by wearing T-shirts and worn denim. In his designer tux, he took her breath away. She had to get away from him before her last brain cell died from lack of oxygen. Officially a member of the wedding party, she had other responsibilities she needed to tend to before she could relax and be the perfect maid of honor Becky deserved for the remainder of the evening.

Removing her hand from his forearm took the last of her willpower. "I've got to check on the dinner," she said, putting distance between them before she gave in and told him everything. "I won't be long."

She'd make a pass through the kitchen while the guests made their way to the front lawn for cocktails under the big tent that had been set up for the occasion. Once she knew the help hired for the night had everything under control, she'd return to the garden to pose for pictures with the bride and groom.

~ ~ ~

Scott stood rooted to the spot as Roseanne entered the house, closing the door with authority. Not exactly slamming it—she'd never disrupt the proceedings in such a way. He loved that she was too much of a lady to let her personal drama intrude on her friend's moment. None of the women who ran in his social circles back home in New York would think twice about creating a scene at another person's wedding.

He wandered back to the rose arbor where the bride and groom posed for photos. For a guy who'd left home for greener pastures, vowing never to return, Ford looked like a proud bull standing in sweet clover. When the photographer called for the groom's parents to join the couple, Scott noticed the momentary lapse in Ford's good mood. His father's death had brought him home to Butte Plains a little over a year ago, and he still grieved the man's passing. If not for the stipulation in the will that Ford keep the family business in operation for twelve months before selling or closing, his friend would never have hung around long enough to get to know the woman he'd just pledged to love, honor, and cherish for the rest of his life.

And I wouldn't have met Roseanne.

Thoughts of the vexing woman should

have soured his mood, but he couldn't help himself where she was concerned. He wanted her. He needed her. He would have her. Again.

Ford's voice cut through the night. "Scott Ramsey! Get your ass over here."

Scott stepped forward. "You sure you want my ugly mug in your pictures? You know you're going to have to look at them for the rest of your life, don't you?"

"He knows," the bride said. "I cautioned him to choose his best man wisely for that very reason."

"And I still chose you, so get over here," Ford said. "Let's get this done so I can dance with my bride."

Scott took his place beside his best friend and smiled for the camera while, inside, his gut churned.

"Hey, Roseanne! Get over here!" Ford waved his hand and yelled over the heads of the guests who'd wandered back, cocktails in hand, to observe.

"I'm coming!" came the breathless reply. Scott hid a juvenile snicker behind his hand.

The crowd parted, allowing Roseanne through, but the moment she breached the front line, she stopped short. The bride and groom weren't alone. Scott Ramsey stood beside Ford, his gaze locked on her. A familiar fire burned there, threatening to reduce her resolve to cinders. Past experience told her it didn't take much to ignite his fire, but she wondered what she'd done this time.

A part of her reveled in the knowledge she affected him so easily—payback for what he did to her. But another part of her realized that women who played with fire often got burned.

"Stand here beside me," Becky urged, sweeping her train behind her with one hand while she held fast to her husband with the other. "We'll get one of the four of us then I want one of you and Scott together."

Oh Lord. She'd expected the photo with the small wedding party, but not the one of her and Scott together. She'd thought she was through touching him for the evening. Would it look strange to put a foot or two of distance between them?

Of course it would. That's why, when the bride and groom stepped from the arbor, she allowed Scott to pull her close with an arm around her waist.

Following the photographer's instructions, they angled slightly so the back of her thigh pressed against the front of Scott's. He placed one hand on her hip, steadying her. Holding her bouquet of pink roses in her hands, she couldn't even swat at Scott's other hand where he'd molded it to her ass.

While the man with the camera fiddled with the lens or some such, Scott leaned in so his warm breath fanned across her neck. "Do you remember the day we met? I wanted you then. I want you even more now."

Roseanne stifled the groan rising in her throat and, hoping to dislodge his hand, shuffled on her feet. All she managed to do was stroke her ass against his wide palm, causing him to grip her hip tighter. "Be still and smile at the camera."

She smiled at the camera, but through the lens of time, she saw the day, the exact moment Fate put this man in her path. She'd been in her office, trying to add two and two and make five, or more, if possible. The sagging economy had reduced business at the B&B to a fickle stream, flush when rain poured down on the citizens of Butte Plains, dry as dust when it didn't. She'd had a full house the week before due to the funeral for Kenneth Adams, Ford's father, but until the next storm, she didn't have a single booking. Then in walked Scott Ramsey, a Viking from the frozen north. A Yankee sent to steal her heart. He'd done that, and so much more.

"All done." The photographer's dismissal sent a wave of relief through her body, but, as she lifted her foot to step from the casual embrace, Scott's arm snaked across her front, dragging her hard against his front. The heavy ridge of his erection pressed against her ass, making her all too aware of her own needs. The very same ones that had landed her in her current predicament.

"I don't want to let you go." His words whispered across her skin. "You want me, too. Don't even try to deny it."

She couldn't. Wouldn't. He'd never believe her anyway. Desire wasn't their problem.

"Let me go," she said, pulling at his wrist. "I've got to get everyone seated so the staff can serve dinner before everything gets cold."

"When this is all over, we need to talk."

For the span of a heartbeat, she thought he knew her secret, but then he gave her rear end a playful slap and said, "Go on, Little Bo Peep. I'll help herd the sheep into the tent."

She went. As fast as possible without spooking the guests into a stampede. Safe inside the kitchen, she willed her racing heart to calm. He couldn't know. He simply wanted to press his case for them being a couple one more time. Perhaps lure her into his bed again. It wouldn't be difficult. It seemed the same hormones that made her weepy and sick also made her horny, and there was no one she wanted to be with except Scott Ramsey. He stirred her libido like no one else ever had—a fact she kept reminding herself was no reason to marry the guy.

Like he would have me. She glanced out the window. Scott made a good sheep dog. Only a few stragglers remained in the garden, but her baby daddy was on the case, rounding them up and steering them to the path leading around to the front yard.

Roseanne turned and held up her hand, fingers splayed. "Five-minute warning. Start with table one and work your way back." She found the head caterer and pulled her aside. "I'll be at table one. If you have any problems or questions, send someone to get me."

"Don't worry about a thing, Ms. Meadows. We've got it under control," the older woman said. "My staff has done this a hundred times or more. You just go. Enjoy the rest of the evening. We'll serve and cleanup then be out of here before you know it."

CHAPTER THIRTEEN

Roseanne did a quick tour inside the tent, making sure the bartenders had everything they needed and that the DJ understood the schedule. Becky's brother, Colin, sang a song during the ceremony that he'd written for the couple and planned to sing a couple more songs—just him and his guitar—after dinner. He was also acting as the Master of Ceremonies.

Satisfied everything was in place, she took her seat next to the bride. Scott occupied the seat on the other side of the groom. Becky and Ford's mother's, Becky's brother, and Ford's aunt rounded out the head table which was covered with a white tablecloth overlaid with shimmering pink taffeta. The bride's bouquet rested in a vase in the center, flanked by smaller arrangements of pink and white roses alternating with pink and white tapers. The other tables were similarly decorated. Crystal stemware and silver flatware reflected light from chandeliers hanging from the tent struts that were strung with pink tulle.

"There you are," Becky said. "I haven't had a chance to thank you for all you've done."

"No thanks necessary."

"Well, you're getting them anyway. Everything is beautiful—just like I knew it would be. Ford and I can't thank you enough."

"She's right," Ford said. "I'm simply amazed. Have you thought about becoming a wedding or event planner? You could do it, you know?"

"That's very nice of you to say, but I've got enough on my plate as it is. Still, if you need my help putting something together for Adams Manufacturing, just let me know. I'll give you the friends and family rate."

"What about me?" Scott said. "Can I get the friends and family rate, too?"

Roseanne caught Becky's curious look but refused to take the bait. "Locals only, Mr. Ramsey."

"What if I was a local? Would I qualify then?"

More than you know. More than you know. Becky kicked her under the table. Roseanne shot her a look meant to silence her. The last thing she needed was Scott picking up on the nonverbal clues flying between her and the bride. He wasn't an idiot. He'd know something was up, and he wouldn't stop until he found out what it was. "Since you aren't then I see no point in speculating."

A team of waiters arrived with their plated meals, and the conversation turned once again to the wedding.

"This is out of this world," Ford said, as he stabbed another slice of Tournedos of Beef Forestiere. "Is this your recipe, Roseanne?"

"Everything on the menu is from one of my recipes." She dipped her fork into her Chateau Potatoes. "I was fortunate to find a caterer who was willing to prepare my recipes instead of insisting on their own."

"I know," Becky said. "The food at these things is usually blah, but oh my God"—she savored a bite of Creamed Carrots and Minted Green Pea Timbales—"this is beyond delicious."

Everyone else at the table complimented the cuisine except Scott who seemed to be attacking his plate like a starving man. Roseanne couldn't think of a better compliment.

"Are you going to put these recipes in your cookbook?" Ford asked. "'Cause, if you are, I'm going to buy Becky a copy."

"Hey!" Becky elbowed her husband. "Are you saying I can't cook?"

"No. I'm saying you can't cook like this." He smiled at his bride, taking the sting out of his words.

Becky shrugged. "He's right. I can barely boil water, much less prepare something this good." She took a sip from her wineglass. "Ford would benefit from the recipes more than I would. He's a great cook."

Scott looked up from his empty plate. "I keep hearing about this cookbook, but I haven't seen it yet. What gives?"

"Roseanne is working on a cookbook," Ford said. "Isn't that right, Roseanne?"

She glanced around the table. All eyes were trained on her. "It's a silly dream," she explained. "I've been querying agents. If I can't find representation, I might self-publish the book."

"What do you need an agent for?" Becky's mom asked.

Roseanne briefly explained what she knew of the publishing industry then turned the conversation back to the bride and groom, where it belonged. Pretty soon, questions about their honeymoon plans were flying, as well as hints from their mothers about the grand babies they hoped would be arriving soon. Roseanne remained silent, picking at the last of her meal. As soon as Ford's mother had brought up the subject of babies, Roseanne had lost her appetite.

Feeling as if someone were watching her, she glanced up. Her gaze collided with Scott's and held.

The waiters returned to clear the empty plates. Colin stood. "That's my cue. Got to get this party started."

Roseanne pushed her chair back. "I'll just make sure the DJ—"

"I've got it, Roseanne," Colin said.

"You're sure?" She sat back down.

"Positive. You just work on your maid-of-honor toast. I'll call you up when it's time."

As instructed, the wait staff delivered individual personalized tissue packs along with coffee and scoops of homemade butter pecan ice cream. Colin took to the stage, and everyone settled in to listen to another original song he'd written for the occasion. He followed that up with a toast to his older sister and her husband. The first tissues came out as he spoke of his sister's unselfishness that allowed him to pursue his love of music while she gave up her dream of working for a large marketing company in a big city. There wasn't a dry eye in the place as the guests lifted glasses of expensive French champagne to the bride's happiness.

Scott took Colin's place at the podium. His eloquent toast spoke of the family we choose as opposed to the family we're born with, emphasizing the fact he thought of Ford as a brother as well as his best friend. Roseanne used the corner of her napkin to collect the tears forming in her eyes as he held his champagne glass aloft. "To friends, the family we choose."

She tipped her glass along with everyone else—only the liquid never met her lips.

Since the men had toasted to the bride and groom individually, Roseanne raised a toast to the couple, wishing both of them a lifetime of love and adventure. As she lifted the champagne flute, she signaled the audio/visual technician. Suddenly, the lights dimmed and a giant screen deployed behind the stage. The guests' reactions were priceless as, one by one, they figured out what they were watching on the screen. When Elvis began to sing "Love Me Tender," a single spotlight lit the center of the dance floor, and in that beam of light, the newlyweds swayed to the music.

Cameras flashed all around, capturing the couple's first dance then Scott took Roseanne's hand and led her to the dance floor. Pretty soon, the parquet square was filled with dancing couples.

As soon as the song ended, the DJ began an instrumental version of the same song, playing it low so everyone could hear the vows Becky and Ford had spoken to each other in Las Vegas. The crowd in the tent cheered when the couple kissed on screen and reenacted the scene right there in the middle of the dance floor surrounded by friends and family.

Roseanne sniffed back tears.

"Here. I saved some of my tissues for you." Scott handed her a nearly full packet of tissues bearing the custom logo Ford had designed for their wedding. "Do you always cry this much at weddings?"

She dabbed at her eyes and used his chest as a shield while she blew her nose. "I don't know. I've only been to two—both of them for Becky and Ford."

"The guests are eating this up," he said. "I was afraid there might be a mutiny when everyone found out they've been married for months."

Ford and Becky were somewhere in the center of the mob that had surrounded them, as the video faded to black, and the date and location of the wedding filled the screen.

"The bride and groom are so happy, everyone has already forgiven them for keeping the secret," Roseanne said.

"I suppose. Can't imagine doing this more than once, though."

Roseanne choked back a sob. She'd dreamed countless times of becoming Scott Ramsey's bride, but no more. The thought of someone else walking down the aisle, speaking sacred vows with him, nearly brought her to her knees. She stumbled. Scott caught her easily, holding her close. "God, I knew this was too much for you. Let's get you to your seat."

"I'm fine," she protested as he

supported almost her entire weight. "I can walk."

"Just let me help you."

She couldn't do otherwise without causing a scene, so she let him half carry her back to their table. As soon as she was seated, he shoved a water glass at her.

"Drink this. Better lay off the champagne until you get some food in your belly."

He'd noticed she'd barely eaten her meal but failed to notice she'd only lifted her champagne glass to her mouth. She hadn't even allowed the liquid to touch her lips. "I was saving room for cake."

"You have someone taking care of the cake cutting, right?"

"Ford and Becky's moms asked if they could be in charge of that. Everything is set up, or it should be."

"I'll check. You sit here." He stood. "What am I looking for? A knife. Some forks and plates?"

"Good grief. It will just take me a second." She stood then gripped the edge of the table as the room began to spin.

"Fuck!" Scott caught her by the elbow and eased her back into her chair. "You aren't going anywhere, unless it's to the hospital."

"I don't need a hospital. I'm fine. I just need to rest a minute."

"You've been overdoing it."

"I have not. It's hot in here, that's all."

"How about a walk in the garden, then? I'll bring you back in time for the cake cutting. I promise."

Roseanne looked around. The DJ had taken over from Colin, and everyone was having a great time, including the bride and groom who were slow dancing to a rock tune that had everyone else bopping around like wind turbines with broken wings. Even Scott's parents were out there, dancing like no one was watching, as the saying went.

"Come on. It's going to be a while before anyone even remembers there's a cake."

Fresh air sounded heavenly. "Okay. But we have to keep an eye on the time. I promised the neighbors the music would be over at a decent hour." She stood slowly, allowing her body time to adjust before she headed for an opening in the panels forming the walls of the tent. Outside, she instantly felt better. Summer nights in Texas couldn't exactly be called cool, but the slight breeze helped.

"Maybe we should open some of the side panels on the tent. I didn't realize how hot it had become until I stepped out here."

"I'll take care of it." He steered her around to the back of the house where the chairs for the ceremony still occupied most of the walkway. "You sit here and don't move until I get back. Promise?"

"I promise. Just get those panels open before someone faints from the heat."

"Will do. Be right back."

CHAPTER FOURTEEN

Roseanne picked up a program that had been left on an adjacent chair and fanned herself. She hadn't been all that hot until Scott had taken her out on the dance floor. It wasn't physical exertion that had heated her blood, but being in his arms. The heat of his body pressed up against hers had sent her libido into overdrive. Couple that with the heat of all those bodies in such close quarters, and you had a recipe for disaster. Lucky for her, Scott was big and strong enough to support her; otherwise, she would have collapsed right there on the dance floor.

She could see it now. Someone would call the paramedics and, before they gave her any meds, she'd have to tell them she was pregnant. Thank goodness Scott hadn't insisted she get medical help; otherwise, her secret would be out, and not in a good way. *I'll tell him. Just not tonight.* No way was she bringing her personal drama out. Absolutely nothing was going to ruin Becky and Ford's big night.

Scott returned with two bottles. He cracked the seal on a bottle of water bearing a pink label that read Becky + Ford and the date surrounded by a heart, and handed it to her before opening the bottle he'd snagged for himself. He sat beside her. "I opened panels on two sides. The air is flowing better now. Everything is fine. I think you can take a few minutes to catch your breath."

"Thanks. I've been going nonstop since early this morning. I guess I didn't realize how hard I'd been pushing myself." She took a sip of water. The cool liquid felt good going down.

"Ford and Becky wouldn't want you to make yourself sick."

"I know. I'm sure I'll be fine. The fresh

air is helping."

Scott took a sip of his beer. "Damn. This is good." He held the bottle up to the light so he could read the label.

"It's called *You're the One*. It was brewed especially for tonight by a local brewer—Lucky Lady Brewery."

He took another swig and smacked his lips. "Never heard of it."

"It's new. I went into McKenna's Liquor store to talk to Mr. McKenna about placing an order for the bars for tonight, and to ask if he could recommend some bartenders. He'd just received a delivery from Lucky Lady. He said the stuff was really good, so I took a couple of bottles to Ford. He loved it, so I contacted the owner to see about getting a supply for tonight."

"How did you get them to brew a special batch for tonight?"

Roseanne shrugged. "The owner is a woman—Julie Davis. When I told her what I needed it for, she offered. Made the special labels and everything for a reasonable price."

"It's excellent for a small batch

brewery." He finished the last of the beer and let out a loud belch.

"Good grief." Roseanne bumped shoulders with him. "At least try to be civilized."

"Why? There's nobody out here but us."

"That was gross."

"That was manly."

"Disgusting." She stifled a laugh. He always knew how to lighten her mood.

"Maybe it was," he conceded. "Sorry."

"Apology accepted."

Ribbing over, their conversation died. Music from the front yard filled the silence between them. Finally, Scott asked, "Tell me about your cookbook."

"I've written one already, and I have enough recipes for several more. I'm trying to find a literary agent, but so far I haven't had any luck. Becky thinks I should self-publish, but I'm not sure I'm up to doing all the work that's involved in something like that. Not and keep the bed-and-breakfast running. I'm going to give it a little more time—see what shakes out—before I decide what to do."

"You're a fabulous cook. I miss the breakfasts you made when I was staying here."

"Thanks. The cook I hired a few months ago is still using my recipes."

"So, not much has changed except that you aren't slaving over a hot stove every morning."

She nodded. "I spend most every afternoon in the kitchen, trying out new recipes and perfecting old ones. I'm sure you've sampled some of my test products. I usually unload them on the unsuspecting employees at Adams Manufacturing."

"That's where all that good stuff in the break room comes from?"

"Yep."

"I'd pay you to drop some of that off at the leather factory. My employees would love it."

"I could do that, but I won't accept payment for it. It's either throw it out, which I can't bear to do, or foist it off on someone else."

"Foist on my employees anytime you want."

"Thanks. I'll do that." Roseanne stood. "I better get back. It's getting late. If I round up the mothers of the bride and groom, can you corral the happy couple? That would save me some time."

"Not a problem. Want me to drag them over to the cake table?"

"If you don't mind."

"Not at all." He put his hand on the small of her back and kept it there as they strolled around to the front yard. The respite had done her good, but the feel of his hand resting possessively on her back reminded her of what they'd once had, and the secret she kept from him. He was a good person, would make an excellent father—if he wanted to. She'd seen the effort he put into getting that old leather factory up and running. If he put even half that much enthusiasm into being a parent, he'd be a good one. But he'd be in New York, and no matter how deeply she believed he'd be a good parent, she couldn't imagine him being a long-distance one.

Inside the tent, she went in search of Ford and Becky's moms. The two of them had inhabited the same city for over two decades, yet they'd never met until recently. From two distinctly different socio-economic groups, they'd orbited the same world, one at the very center, the core, the other on the periphery, so insignificant as to be invisible. Now, they were on equal footing by virtue of their children marrying. As Roseanne watched them collaborate on the details of the cake-cutting ceremony, she couldn't tell which one had traveled the farthest to get to where they were now. They made it look easy, the woman who had been born to wealth, and the one who had scraped by even in the best of times, working together for a common goal— grandkids.

Neither one had been discreet about their wishes. Both widowed, their children grown, they were ready for grandparenthood.

~ ~ ~

Scott spotted his prey. He wove his way through the crowd on the dance floor to where Ford and Becky held court. They looked exhausted but deliriously happy at the same time. He hated to be the one to tell them the night was almost over, but someone had to. This shindig couldn't go on forever. He tapped his best friend on the shoulder.

"You trying to cut in?" Ford asked.

"I would, but Roseanne said it's time to cut the cake."

"Already?" Becky asked. "Seems like we just had dinner."

"That was over an hour ago," Scott said. "The natives are getting restless. They want cake."

"Then, let them eat cake," Ford said, taking his bride by the hand. "Lead the way. We'll follow."

Scott cleared a path to a table set up near the stage. Draped in the same shimmering pink tulle as the guests' tables, it was topped with a huge, four-tiered cake. A ribbon made up of real pink roses cascaded across the top layer and wound down and around to the bottom, reminiscent of the bride's classic gown which gave way in back to a long, ruffled train.

Mrs. Adams and Mrs. Parker teamed

up to toast the couple then stepped aside to let them cut the cake.

"Thanks for getting them over here." Roseanne appeared at his side.

"No problem. Where'd you go?"

"I ran to the bathroom. All that water."

Scott chuckled. "At least you aren't dehydrated."

Ford and Becky took turns smashing cake into the other's mouth. As usual, everyone cheered and laughed at the ridiculous custom. Scott knew if he ever got to smear frosting and cake anywhere on the woman at his side, he'd make every effort to lick it all off. From the look on Ford's face, he was having the exact same thought regarding his bride.

"I'm hungry, though. I've had my eye on that cake ever since the bakery delivered it this afternoon. I can't wait to find out if it's as delicious as it looks."

"It does look good." He applauded along with everyone else as the couple intertwined their arms and sipped from champagne flutes engraved with Mr. and Mrs. "Why don't you go sit at the table? I'll grab us a couple of slices."

"Thanks." She walked away.

He'd never seen her look so tired. Maybe it was the stress of putting on such a big event, or that coupled with the heat, but he planned to keep an eye on her. He'd find some excuse to check on her tomorrow, and if she wasn't looking better, she was going to see a doctor. That was all there was to it. He dodged the newlyweds and snagged two slices of cake. He waved off the filled flutes offered to him and grabbed another beer for himself and a water bottle for Roseanne from the bar.

Roseanne was alone at the table. Scott could account for everyone except Colin. He hadn't seen Becky's brother since the video had ended. He'd probably snuck out to meet old friends or something.

"Here you go." He held out the drinks. "Water or beer?"

"I think I'd better stick with water." She took both bottles, placing the beer on his side.

"Probably a good idea," he said as he handed her a plate and fork. "I've got a feeling there are going to be a lot of people here who are going to wish they'd made the same decision come morning."

Roseanne laughed. "Don't you know it? Have you taken a look at the liquor bottles at the bars? A lot of them are almost empty. They weren't small bottles, either."

"And that doesn't take into consideration the amount of champagne and beer that's been consumed."

"True."

They ate in silence for a few minutes then Scott asked, "Is the cake as good as you thought it would be?"

Roseanne forked up another bite. "It's fabulous. I wasn't sure the bakery could duplicate my recipe for such a large batch, but they did a great job I think."

"This is your recipe, too?"

"You like it?"

"It's incredible. I've been to dozens of weddings, and, to be honest, I usually pass on the cake. They're like eating sawdust. I have to say, I'm surprised."

"I'm just full of surprises, Scott Ramsey."

He smiled and took a drink from his beer. "I'm sure you are, Roseanne Meadows. I'm sure you are."

CHAPTER FIFTEEN

Scott sighed. He'd lost track of Roseanne again. She'd nibbled at her cake then excused herself to check on some minor detail. Wandering the tent, looking for her, he almost ran into Ford who had somehow become separated from Becky. "Have you seen Becks?"

"No. Have you seen Roseanne?"

"Can't say that I have." The groom shoved an empty beer bottle into Scott's hand. "Take this, would you? I need to find my bride and drag her out on the dance floor again before the DJ packs it in for the night."

"Don't you have a plane to catch?" Scott looked around for a place to ditch the empty bottle.

Still searching the crowd, Ford said, "Thanks to a very generous friend who loaned us his private jet, we don't have to rush. He assured me the plane wouldn't leave without us."

"Just bring my plane back in one piece, and you're responsible for cleaning the interior if necessary."

Ford smirked. "Thank goodness the seats are leather."

"Go on. Find Becky and dance the night away if you want. The jet will be waiting whenever you get there. Oh, and if I haven't already said it, congratulations. I wish you all the best."

"Thanks, man. I always thought 'the one' was a myth, but Becky changed my mind." With that, he headed off like a man on a mission. Scott silently wished him well.

A few couples remained on the dance floor, some more skilled than others. Snagging another of the craft brews from the bar set up in the corner, he took a satisfying swig. Whoever the owner of Lucky Lady was, she knew how to brew a good beer. It wouldn't take much to expand the business well beyond the confines of Butte Plains, if she chose to do so.

Why wouldn't she? The business man in him calculated the profits to be made with wide distribution and came up with a number sure to entice any entrepreneur. He sure as hell planned to go wide with his leather goods. He'd signed a contract with Ford and Becky to feature his line of apparel and implements for the BDSM lifestyle through their home shopping network. Next week, he'd be meeting with a popular brick and mortar retailer about carrying his more mainstream products in their stores. Add in his own direct-purchase system, and the sales projections were through the roof.

A murmur swept through the crowd. Scott looked up in time to see the bride and groom take to the dance floor. Scott smiled to himself. Ford had found his woman; it was time he did the same.

He set the empty beer bottle on a service table near the rear entry then made his way down the worn red-brick path that wound around the side of the house to the gardens where the ceremony had taken place. The tiny white lights Roseanne had strung through the branches of the century-old oaks twinkled in the occasional soft breeze, reminding him of Central Park in the summer. Adding to the ambiance, candles in jelly jars dotted the gardens, peeking out from under rose bushes and summer blooms he couldn't begin to identify. Everything about the simple décor screamed romance.

Scott stopped on the pathway, turned, and scanned the back of the house. Lovely in its old age, the Victorian had nothing on its owner who stood silhouetted in the wavy handmade glass of the kitchen window. Roseanne belonged here, in this place, and in this time. She loved the old house she'd inherited from her grandmother, and the house loved her, if that were possible. She nurtured it, and, as if to say thank you, it sparkled like a gem for her.

He blinked, and when he looked again, she'd moved off to take care of some other imagined emergency or such. She'd eventually come back outside, if for no other reason than to snuff the candles. Deciding to wait for her, he crammed his hands in the trouser pockets of his tuxedo and strolled the path.

"The party is in the front yard, Mr. Ramsey."

At the sound of her voice, Scott spun to face the woman he couldn't get out of his system. She stood a safe distance away, but close enough he could make out the lines of fatigue bracketing her eyes and her mouth. He wanted nothing more than to sweep her into his arms and carry her away so he could take care of her.

He smiled, hoping the darkness prevented her from seeing the raw need that had to be obvious on his face. "I thought you were coming right back. Is everything okay inside?"

She nodded. "We're almost out of beer, but we have enough champagne to fill a swimming pool, so I told the staff to push that a little harder."

"The beer is very popular. I hope you kept a case back for Ford and Becky to take home."

"I kept two, actually. Locked them up in the cellar." She glanced toward the path leading around the house. "I need to go check on things in the tent, see if I can move things along."

He fell into step beside her, and they made their way around to the front yard. "Are they doing the traditional garter-and-bouquet-throwing thing, or are they bucking tradition once again?"

"Despite the Vegas wedding, they're very traditional people. Why don't you see if you can round up some single men, and I'll round up the single women, and maybe we can get this show on the road?"

Scott mock saluted her. "Will do."

He couldn't take his eyes off her. She seemed to have gotten a second wind, bustling about, herding the guests like a true cowhand so they didn't even realize they had no choice. Her cheeks flushed from the heat and exertion, and he couldn't help but remember when she'd had that look for an entirely different reason. Lord, what she'd done to him. He couldn't get her out of his mind, or his heart.

She'd wrangled the crowd to form a corral of sorts with the bride and groom in the center then taken her place along the rail to watch the age-old custom of stealing a garter from the bride.

Scott stood in the center of the small group of unattached bachelors he'd gathered, watching.

Becky looked like she'd rather crawl under the nearest table than bare her leg for everyone to see, but Ford wasn't going to be denied. Seating her like a queen in the chair Scott had placed center stage, Ford dropped to one knee in front of his bride. Their gazes locked. Ford lifted her foot, caressed her ankle. The onlookers cheered him on as his hands crept beneath her gown, slowly advancing toward his goal. The two seemed locked in their own intimate world, completely oblivious to the fact that several dozen people watched their every move. What should have been a light moment had become a sensual testament to the couple's connection.

Realizing he'd been holding his breath, Scott forced the air from his lungs, and, feeling guilty for watching such an intimate exchange, he sought out Roseanne. One hand pressed to her heart, she dabbed at the corners of her eyes with a tissue. She'd seen it, too, that almost magical bond the bride and groom shared. *Look at me, sweetheart. Look at me.* As if she'd heard his thoughts, she scanned the circle, coming to a stop on him. Heart hammering, he met her gaze. *We have it, too. We have it, too.*

Wolf whistles erupted all around him. He looked up just in time to see something flying through the air. Instinct took over. He put his arm up to shield himself. Someone jostled him to the side. His arm lowered to protect his body from the new, closer threat. Something brushed against his hand. His fingers closed into a fist, trapping the offending object a split-second before he realized what he'd captured. His gaze went to his hand, to the scrap of blue satin and white lace peeking out between his fingers. *Shit.*

The other single men clapped him on the shoulder, congratulating him on a job well-done. Several off-color remarks were made, but all he could think about was that, in a few minutes, he'd be taking Ford's place in the center of the circle in order to place the bride's garter on the leg of a yet-to-be-selected single woman. There was no hope for it; he had to go along with the silly custom. Smiling, he tucked the garter halfway into his breast pocket, letting it dangle out for all to see. The guests cheered the move before turning their attention once again to the bride and groom.

Across the circle of guests, Roseanne assembled the single women into a knot. Amid cheers and whistles, Becky tossed her bouquet over her shoulder. It soared in a high arc, coming down in the midst of the group. Fingers grasped and came up empty as the pink nosegay defied their best attempts to snag it. Scott lost sight of it as it dropped behind the head of one of the taller women. Gasps and groans from the assembly told him someone had finally managed to get their hands on the flying flowers. As the group parted, gently shoving the woman with the winning hand to the front, Scott once again held his breath.

Someone shoved him forward. He stumbled, righted himself, and looked up. He saw her feet first. Strappy silver sandals gave way to trim ankles and shapely calves that disappeared under a tea-length pink skirt. His gaze traveled up to where the bride's delicate, pink bouquet shook in the woman's hands. Hands that had driven him crazy more times than he could count. Hands he desperately wanted to feel on him again.

Roseanne. He smiled.

CHAPTER SIXTEEN

Oh, shit.

Roseanne eyed the roses she hadn't meant to catch. Somehow, they'd ended up in her hands anyway. Stunned, she allowed the others to shove her toward the front.

Becky squealed with delight then rushed over to grab her in a bear hug. "I'm so happy! Go get him, girlfriend!"

Roseanne forced a smile to her lips. She'd rather eat the bouquet than allow Scott Ramsey to place that garter on her leg in front of all these people, but she had no choice. This was Becky's big day, and she wouldn't ruin it for her.

"Okay. Okay. Give me some room."

She wiggled out of the bride's embrace. Striding across the open floor was the one man she was genetically programmed to want. Too handsome for words, especially in his custom-tailored tux, she felt her resolve vaporizing.

"Hurry up," Becky urged, giving her a little shove. "The sooner you get this over with, the sooner I can get on with the honeymoon."

And the sooner Scott goes back into his hole.

Okay. I've got this.

She forced her feet to move toward the chair in the center of the room. Scott met her halfway, extending his hand. Steeling herself for his touch, she placed her fingers on his palm. The electric current she'd come to expect when they touched hummed through her body. Her heartbeat ratcheted into the stratosphere while the blood coursing through her arteries thickened to molten lava.

"I've got you, sweetheart."

Her eyes met his. The desire she saw there had to mirror her own, yet, like a moth drawn to the flame, she couldn't look away, couldn't save herself. She'd known the second she saw the bouquet in her hands that she was going down, that she didn't have the fortitude to resist him if he put his hands on her again.

She let him guide her to the chair. Clutching the roses hard enough to crush the stems, she sat. Dimly aware of the catcalls and cheering going on around them, she couldn't tear her gaze away from Scott. He didn't seem to notice their audience any more than she did as he went down on one knee in front of her. His fingers closed around her ankle, a warm, tender shackle that made her weak with need. In his eyes, she saw recognition. He, too, recalled the times she'd lay naked and open to him while he placed the restraints on her ankles and wrists.

"Relax, baby." He held her ankle fast with one hand while the other reached for the garter dangling like some erotic trophy from his breast pocket. "I'll take care of you."

His promise, spoken only for her ears, went straight to her most tender spots.

She gripped the seat of the chair with her free hand to keep from squirming.

Gaze locked with hers, he maneuvered the elastic band over her foot then slowly, with both hands, inched it past her ankle, over her calf. She held her breath as his fingers scorched a path over her knee to her thigh, pausing there. Hidden beneath her skirt, his hands branded her skin, claimed the sensitive flesh as his own. The heat in his eyes guaranteed the promise his hands made.

One more time. What would it hurt? She craved to feel the press of his skin against hers one last time. Needed to know the touch of another human being, know the heat and urgency of desire.

Slowly, his hands retraced the path they'd taken, until her foot once again rested on the floor. Eyes still locked with hers, he rose and placed his lips on hers. Just a gentle brush of warm skin on numb skin, but it brought a cheer from the crowd and snapped Roseanne out of her lust-induced coma. She jerked when his lips brushed the shell of her ear. "Your room in five. If you aren't there, I'll come looking for you."

What else could she do? She nodded. Taking her by the elbow, he drew her to her feet. With his arm supporting her waist, they smiled and waved at the cheering crowd.

Becky rushed forward, placing a kiss on her cheek. "We're going to go change clothes. See you in a few?"

Roseanne nodded. "Take your time."

"You okay?" Scott asked.

"Yeah." She twisted out of his embrace. "I need to check on something in the house."

"I'll come with you."

She dropped the bridal bouquet on the small table in the hallway then they took the back stairs to avoid any guests who might wander into the house. The DJ had put on a dance favorite that probably kept most of them occupied, but Roseanne wasn't in the mood for interruptions. On the second landing, Scott caught up to her. Putting his hand possessively on her ass, he propelled them to the third floor.

She opened the door. He kicked it

shut behind them at the same time his arm snaked around her waist, pulling her back flush against his front.

"Got to have you." The words rumbled from his chest, the vibration equally as arousing as the words themselves.

"Oh, God." She'd lost her mind, but she didn't miss it one little bit. Her body fit itself to his, muscle memory and longing making her pliable.

His free hand found her nape. His fingers worked their way around to her jaw while his thumb exerted pressure on the back of her head. She dipped her chin to her chest. With her hair piled high in a fancy updo, he had full access to the sensitive skin on the back of her neck. He pressed an openmouthed kiss below her ear. A shiver ran down her spine. "You taste so good. I could eat you up."

She groaned, imagining him doing just that. "Please." If she didn't get relief soon she'd combust.

"On the bed." They crossed the distance together then he spun her around and took her face in his big hands. His heated gaze said it all, and hers answered back, lowering to his lips. He took her mouth in a kiss that sent the lava in her bloodstream rocketing along. She reached out, grabbed fistfuls of starched cotton to ground herself. It didn't work. Her head spun and her hips moved, seeking the hard ridge beneath his fly. His lips left hers. "Sweet Jesus, I've got to taste you."

She nodded. He lifted her like she weighed nothing and tossed her on the bed. Wishing they had time for restraints, she grabbed for the footboard, holding on as he pushed her skirt to her waist. A low growl came from his throat then he reached for her panties. They were gone in an instant. He shoved her thighs apart, opening her to his gaze. "Fucking beautiful," he said.

He lowered himself between her legs. The first brush of warm breath against her skin had her bucking her hips off the bed. Knowing she needed to cede control, he seized it. Wrapping his arms around her thighs, he yanked her to the edge of the mattress and buried his face in her pussy.

She cried out and, closing her eyes, gave herself over to the incredible sensations created by his talented lips and tongue. He knew how to drive her wild with need, drawing his tongue over her swollen flesh, slow and easy, until every nerve ending in her body tingled then flicking her clit or thrusting deep inside her. She clutched the footboard with one hand and the quilt top with the other as he took her to the peak and beyond.

Pleasure, sharp and oh, so glorious, shot through her. Her body convulsed, fought his firm but gentle restraint until, at last, the crisis passed and she floated back to earth. She felt his smile against her thigh as he placed a sweet kiss there, just inches away from her core.

Like he had all the time in the world, he stood and carefully smoothed her skirt back over her wet center. "These are mine," he said. She blinked tears from her eyes and, in the dim moonlight streaming in the window, saw her panties dangling from his index finger. "You can keep the garter."

Her circumstances hit her like a sledgehammer. A tent full of people were on her front lawn. The bride and groom had gone to change into travel clothes, and, instead of handing out origami doves filled with birdseed, she'd selfishly been playing hanky-panky with the best man!

"I've got to go." She pushed herself upright.

"Roseanne." He blocked her way.

"No." She shook her head. Lord, she must look a mess. "This was a mistake."

"You don't really believe that."

She placed her hands on his stomach and shoved. "Get out of my way, Scott. I've got to go."

He stepped back. She sprang for the door, but before she convinced the temperamental old doorknob to turn, his words slammed into her. "This isn't over, Roseanne. *We* aren't over."

Yes, we are. Her feet pounded on the back stairs to the rhythm of her heartbeat. She hit the last landing and sprinted for the powder room off the front hall, praying that none of her guests were using it. She'd be screwed if someone saw her this way—eyes filled with tears, lips swollen, hair probably a rat's nest, and sporting a full-body blush. There'd be no doubt what she'd been up to, and anyone who knew her would know who she'd been up to it with.

The gods must have been watching out for her. She dashed into the powder room, locked the door, and faced herself in the mirror. "Dear God."

It took her a good ten minutes to finger-comb her hair into some semblance of normality and another five to erase the raccoon smudges under her eyes. Her dress had a few more wrinkles than before, but all in all looked pretty good—considering. She wished she'd thought to grab a fresh pair of panties, but she hadn't. Only one person would know she wasn't wearing any, and if he so much as smirked at her, she'd hit him over the head with a chair.

When she finally emerged from the powder room, she found Ford and Becky waiting in the front parlor to make their grand escape.

"We were wondering where you were," the bride said. "Is everything okay?"

"Fine," she lied. "If you'll just give me a minute, I'll make sure everyone is ready to send you off in style."

"Can't we just skip this part and disappear out the back door?" Ford asked.

"No, you can't skip this part," Roseanne said. "If they don't see you leave, they'll stay here all night, and I promised the neighbors we'd shut this down before midnight."

"He's kidding." Becky gave her groom a kiss on the cheek. "Aren't you, darling?"

Ford shrugged. "Sure. Just kidding, Roseanne."

His reluctant acquiescence amused her. She smiled and held up a finger. "Give me a minute. I'll come open the door for you when we're all ready."

She ducked out, closed her eyes, and breathed in the fresh, night air, willing it to settle her nerves. When she opened her eyes, Scott stood in the open tent panel, hands in his pockets, staring at her. "Are they ready?"

Roseanne nodded. "Yes. I have the birdseed packets here." She pointed to a couple of baskets filled with the paper birds she'd left on the porch swing.

"I'll tell the DJ to make the announcement." He turned and headed into the tent. Helping her, despite the way she'd ran out on him.

Placing a hand on her stomach, she refused to think about how she'd left him. He'd given her an explosive orgasm, and she'd given him nothing. Yet here he was, helping her bring the evening to a conclusion. Maybe Becky was right. Maybe she should tell him tonight.

When the last guests had departed, she expected to see him waiting for her, but he was nowhere to be found.

CHAPTER SEVENTEEN

Roseanne opened the refrigerator and groaned. She'd tried her best to forget about catching the bride's bouquet, but she couldn't deny the evidence. Someone, probably the caterer, had put the flowers in the refrigerator to preserve them. Damn Becky for insisting Roseanne take part in the ridiculous tradition. Folks in Butte Plains took that kind of crap seriously.

The best she could hope for would be that everyone who saw her catch the bundle of pink roses would be unable to recall anything that happened last evening. Otherwise, everyone in town would know about her misfortune before the tent came down later today. The Butte Plains grapevine worked that fast. Thank God no one knew what had happened *after* the spectacle on the dance floor.

Roseanne groaned. How stupid could she be? But she'd never been able to resist Scott when he looked at her the way he had when he slipped the garter onto her leg. His kiss had incinerated her last bit of willpower. No more. She'd made that clear afterward. He'd caught her at a vulnerable moment—that was all. She'd succumbed to his charm, to the sexy way he growled when he kissed her. Damn. Why had he done that? He'd known she would melt.

Moving the flowers aside, she found the carton of milk she had come looking for. Taking it out, she shut the refrigerator door, blocking the blooms from sight. It was early. Jamie wouldn't be in to begin prepping for breakfast for at least another hour. Hopefully, her guests would sleep in. Ford's aunt had turned in right after the wedding cake had been served. Mr. and Mrs. Ramsey had danced until the very last note of the very last song before calling it a night. If there was one thing those two were good at, it was partying. According to their son, they had plenty of experience.

She had no idea what time Colin had gone to bed. She'd lost track of him right after the DJ took over. He was a grown man, and thus, not her responsibility. He could do as he pleased. She just wished he'd been there to see the bride and groom off on their honeymoon. If Becky had noticed his absence, she hadn't said anything. She'd been excited to get on the plane Scott had provided to take them to Paris. She'd also had a lot to drink, like most of the guests. Well, she had ten days ahead of her. Plenty of time to get over a hangover and still see the sights.

A knock on the back door startled her, causing her to spill the milk she'd been pouring into a glass. She turned. Through the window, she recognized her early morning caller.

Colin Parker, his bow tie hanging loose and his tuxedo jacket slung over his shoulder, smiled. "Hey, Roseanne. I forgot my key. Can you let me in?"

Hands on her hips, she frowned at him. He'd abandoned his sister on her wedding night only to come prowling home like a satisfied tomcat the next morning, begging for forgiveness.

"Ah, come on, Roseanne. Let me in."

She flicked the dead bolt—all the help she was going to give him—and stepped back. He twisted the handle and stepped inside.

"Thanks. I've been sitting out there for hours, waiting for someone to wake up." He opened the refrigerator and stared inside just like he used to do when he was a kid and followed his sister everywhere, including to Roseanne's grandmother's house. "Not many leftovers," he commented.

"That's a good thing. There's plenty of cake." She motioned to a couple of large boxes stacked on the corner near the coffeemaker. "It's good. You should try it."

Colin groaned and shut the refrigerator door. "Did she notice I wasn't there for the cake?"

Roseanne shook her head. "I don't think so, but she'll eventually see the pictures." Meaning he wouldn't be in any of them.

"She won't hold that against me. She knew I wanted to see some old friends while I was here."

"Your friends only come out at night? Is that why you couldn't have waited until today?"

He popped the lid on the top box, eyed the contents then opened cabinets until he found a plate.

"There's a knife in the wood block to your right. Forks are in the drawer right behind you in the island."

He nodded. "Same place they were when we were kids." He plopped a generous slice of cake on his plate then licked his fingers before opening the drawer containing the flatware.

"Same flatware, too."

He examined the fork he'd chosen. "I'll be damned. Sure looks the same."

"Where were you?"

"Went to see some old buddies of

mine. You remember the Watson twins? Bobby and Tommy?"

"I thought they were in jail."

He shook his head as he chewed then swallowed. "Not anymore. They own a music store now. All legit. You've seen it. Music City over on Woodlawn?"

"That's their place?" Recently opened, they sold musical instruments, gave lessons, and hosted local talent on a stage out back on weekends. Even without a liquor license, the place had become very popular. "Explains why they don't sell alcohol at their events."

"They served their time and learned their lesson. Maybe they'll never have a liquor license, but they don't need one. Place was hoppin' last night."

"I'm sure it was." She drank the last of her milk then rinsed and put the glass in the dishwasher.

"I just came down to check that everything was okay for my cook to come in and make breakfast this morning. Looks like the caterers did a good job of cleaning up, so I'm going back to bed for a few hours." She pointed a finger at her guest who she loved as if he was her own little brother. "Don't you dare leave your mess for Jamie to clean up." She turned to leave.

"Hey. Wait a sec."

The serious tone of his voice stopped her. She leaned against the newel post on the back stairs. "What?"

"I met someone last night. Name's Julie Davis. You know her?"

"I've heard of her. Why?"

Colin shrugged. "Just wondering. She's new in town, right?"

"She's been here about a year, I think. Bought the Scoggins' place when they retired from farming and turned it into a boutique brewery. Did you have beer at the reception?"

"Yeah. That was hers?"

"Yep." She put her foot on the next step. "That's all I know about her. Remember what I said about leaving a mess." She climbed the stairs to her room on the third floor. By the time her head hit the pillow, she'd forgotten all about Colin staying out all night and his questions about the owner of Lucky Lady

The Yankee Billionaire's Bride

Brewing Company.

CHAPTER EIGHTEEN

Fuck.

Scott had spent yet another restless night, thinking about the few moments he'd had alone with Roseanne. He hadn't meant for things to go that far, but the volcano had been stirring for two days. Seeing and touching her, even innocently at the rehearsal, had been the catalyst, setting his blood on fire—reminding him of exactly what he'd lost.

Looking like a sweet, pink confection last night, she'd made his mouth water. Everyone could have their addictions— alcohol, nicotine, name your drug. Roseanne was his addiction. He lived to touch, smell, taste her. He'd been in withdrawal since she'd come to her senses and kicked him out of her life. He didn't deserve her. It had been only a matter of time before she figured it out.

She'd forgotten for a few minutes last night, and so had he. He'd earned the blue balls he'd suffered most of the night. He should have kept his hands to himself, should never have followed her up those stairs. Should never have let his needs overrule his brain. But if last night turned out to be his last memory of the way she sounded when he made her come, of the heaven between her legs, he'd cherish it until his dying day.

But today was another day in his quest to be the man he wanted to be. Even if Roseanne never saw him as anything more than a Yankee carpetbagger, he'd do what he could to make her town the place she envisioned. There was no time to lose. He needed to find the right tenants for the buildings downtown, and if nothing else had come from last night, he'd had an idea.

He'd spent the morning researching his prey. He'd been surprised to find very little about the owner of Lucky Lady Brewing Company. The people he'd talked to all said she wasn't a local and that she kept to herself. No one knew where she came by the funds to buy the property she occupied or to start up a microbrewery. That didn't mean the Butte Plains grapevine wasn't ripe with speculation, but Scott wasn't interested in imaginative guesswork.

Scott consulted the GPS one more time. A large, white barn with a green shingled roof loomed in the distance next to a smaller, but every bit as impressive, farmhouse. He slowed, checked the number on the oversized mailbox perched on top of the stump of what had once been a very large tree. It had taken some investigative work, but he'd eventually located the old Scoggins place, which meant he'd found the home of the Lucky Lady Brewing Company. He flicked the turn signal on, and, with a whispered prayer that the homeowner didn't shoot trespassers, he crept up the driveway.

As he approached the house, a large,

black dog bounded out from the shade of a century-old oak to meet his car. He didn't know much about dogs, but this one, with its wagging tail and lolling tongue, appeared friendly enough. Scott parked next to a vintage pickup truck that bore the logo he'd become familiar with, and cut the engine. When no one greeted him with a shotgun, he decided his luck was holding.

"So far, so good," he muttered as he opened the car door.

It wasn't the first time he'd questioned his sanity regarding everything Butte Plains, Texas. He'd risked a small fortune on the leather factory, the old, abandoned airstrip, and still another on the real estate downtown. Thanks to Ford and Becky's success with Adams Manufacturing, vacant properties were being snatched up by savvy investors, and he'd plunked the money down before considering what he would do with the extra square footage. He intended to use the Cotton Exchange building for his new offices. One space would become the new offices of Ramsey and Adams

Designs. He had plans for the space between the Cotton Exchange and the corner, but the way things were going, he wasn't sure they would ever get off the ground. That left the corner property, and, after last night, he knew exactly what he wanted to occupy the space. According to the few people who knew the brewer, the chances of convincing her to open a tasting room in his vacant location were roughly the same as an armadillo crossing a freeway without getting run over. In other words—nil.

When no one answered the door at the house, Scott followed his nose around the beautiful old structure to the barn he'd seen from the road. The friendly black lab trudged along behind him as he traversed the well-worn path that led to a pedestrian door on the west side. Through the multi-paned window, he could see most of the operation inside. He knocked. He was about to give up and try again another day, when a woman appeared in the window. If this was Julie Davis, she was much younger than he'd thought—mid-twenties, he'd guess. Younger than him by half a decade, at least. He smiled and waved.

A striking woman, she looked comfortable in jeans and a pastel plaid shirt left open to reveal some sort of girly white undershirt thing. She wore athletic shoes, and had her long, blonde hair up in a ponytail that swung back and forth as she strode toward the door. The scowl on her face when she jerked the door open wasn't a good sign.

"Yes?" she said, keeping one hand on the doorknob while the other held a clipboard against her chest.

Scott wasn't sure if her displeasure stemmed from the interruption or from having company in general. More than one person had described the woman as a recluse. He wondered if her lack of community interaction had more to do with being busy than anything else. He'd never given much thought to the brewing process, but what he could see of this small operation looked like a lot of work for one person.

He held out his hand. "Scott Ramsey, Ms. Davis?"

She dipped her head in acknowledgement but made no effort to shake his hand. "I'm Julie Davis."

So this was the owner of Lucky Lady Brewery—a Texan if her soft drawl was genuine, and he believed it was. He'd long since learned the slow dialect had nothing to do with the person's intelligence. Something in her tone warned him not to underestimate her. He dropped his hand to his side.

"What brings you all the way out here, Mr. Ramsey?"

"I was wondering if I could have a minute of your time. I have a business proposition I'd like to discuss with you."

She glanced at her clipboard then looked over her shoulder. His gaze followed hers to a giant tank. Steam rose from a large open hatch on the top. "Look, I don't know what you're selling, but I'm not buying. Now, if you'll excuse me? I've got to keep an eye on the temperature of that vat."

"What I've got to say will only take a minute," he pressed. "Could you monitor the vat and listen at the same time?"

She rolled her eyes at him then swung the door open wide. She pointed a finger at the dog. "No, Bud. Wait." The dog, tongue hanging out and tail wagging, sat. She turned her attention back to Scott and gestured for him to enter. "Come on. I don't have time to argue with you."

Scott stepped inside and was immediately hit with a wall of humid air, thick with the smell of something earthy. He took in the impressive facility. Clearly, there was more to brewing beer than cooking up some hops, or whatever it was they used. Besides the dozen or so giant stainless steel vats and tanks, he noted a small bottling station to one side. A stack of flattened cardboard sat next to what he assumed was a labeler. One entire wall of the place from floor to ceiling was lined with industrial shelving, on which sat pallets stacked with supplies. He noticed a small forklift parked in the corner. He might not know the brewing business, but recognized expense when he saw it. Ms. Davis had spent a lot of her, or someone else's, money on her equipment. As he made his way over to where the owner of the Lucky Lady Brewing Company stood, he wondered if she considered this a business, or if she was just another rich girl with a hobby.

"Nice place," he said.

She consulted a couple of gauges on a panel then glanced at her clipboard again. "Talk, Mr. Ramsey, or leave. I'm busy."

Scott raised one eyebrow at the curt comment and cleared his throat. "Like I said, I have a business proposition for you."

"Go on," she said, not taking her eyes off the steaming vat. "Just be ready to move fast. That's boiling water in there. Sometimes it splashes over."

She didn't move, and, not wanting to look like a wimp, neither did he. "Are you familiar with the Cotton Exchange building downtown?"

"I've seen it. Looks like it was an impressive place back in the day."

"I own it, and the buildings on either side of it. I'm moving my offices into the Exchange building. I'm thinking the corner space would make a good tasting room for Lucky Lady."

The side glance she gave him might have meant anything from she was interested, to wishing him to hell. At long last, she focused her attention on the gauges again. She hadn't ordered him to leave, so he waited with one eye on the open hatch, from which boiling water could erupt at any second, and the woman who controlled the micro-universe he'd entered. After a minute or two, she jotted something down on her clipboard and turned to him.

"What makes you think I'd want to open a tasting room?"

He nodded at the row of stainless steel vats. "This looks like a pretty expensive hobby."

"It's not a hobby."

"I know less than nothing about this business, but I do know you can't be making money on the volume you're currently producing and selling. At best, that's a failing business model. You have an excellent product, and this town is in need of a place for folks to unwind.

Recent notoriety is bringing tourists and people looking to relocate. Now would be a great time to hitch your wagon to the train before it leaves the station."

She smiled and turned to study her gauges. He got the impression she wasn't an impulsive person. *Wonder what brought her here? Why a brewery?* At last, she spoke. "If I wanted to hitch my wagon to anything, it wouldn't be a train, at least not the kind that leaves a station. You aren't from around here, are you?"

"New York. But I live here now."

She nodded. "Carpetbagger?"

He bristled. "No." Shook his head. "Hell, no."

"Gonna take more than that to convince me otherwise."

What is it with the women in this town? Maybe he should take an ad out in the local paper, listing his references and his intention to become a permanent resident. Maybe then she'd believe he wasn't trying to take advantage of her or the people of Butte Plains. "You provided the beer for Ford Adams's wedding. I was the best man. Ford and I are partners on several business ventures and friends. We met at MIT, went into business together in New York. He can vouch for me."

"The Adams family goes back a long ways in this town."

"They do." He nodded. "Oldest and biggest employer in town."

She sighed and wrote another note on her clipboard. "Look, I can't say I'm not interested in expanding, but I'm busy right now. Can we talk another time?"

"Sure. No problem." He fished a business card out of his wallet and handed it to her. "Call me when you have some time. I'll give you a tour of the space then we can sit down and talk about the details—rent, renovations, marketing."

She slid the card beneath the spring-loaded clamp on her clipboard. "I could spare some time in the next week or so. I'll give you a call."

"Thanks." He took another look around and decided he needed to do some research on the brewing process before they met again. "I'll just let myself out."

While he waited for the brewer to grant him an audience, Scott kept busy with the other projects he had going on—anything to keep from knocking on Roseanne's door and begging her to reconsider. He believed in the old saying, actions speak louder than words. When Julie Davis finally did call several weeks later, they met downtown the next morning. "It doesn't look like much," he said as he worked on the old lock, willing it to open. "But it's solid. I've had two different engineers look over every inch of the place. If you're okay with keeping the historic look, then everything else is just cosmetic."

The door gave way, and he allowed Julie to precede him. There was just enough light coming through dirty windows to illuminate the dust particles they'd stirred up.

CHAPTER NINETEEN

The owner of the Lucky Lady Brewery stood in the middle of the big front room and slowly spun in a circle, taking in the ancient hardwood floors, the wide expanse of windows and the tin-clad ceiling. "What was this originally?"

"Records show the first tenant was a general store. They went out of business around the beginning of the century, the twentieth century," he clarified. "After that, a women's dry-goods store moved in. They occupied the space for nearly eighty years before calling it quits. A couple of small stores tried to make a go of it here over the next few decades, the last being a floor tile business that closed ten years ago."

"So, the space has been vacant since the turn of the century? The twenty-first century?"

"That's right."

"What's going to happen to it if I don't open a tasting room in the space?"

Scott shrugged. "I don't know. I'll have to find something else to put in here. Maybe a restaurant or an old-fashioned soda fountain. It needs to be something that will bring people this far off the freeway to sit for a while, maybe stroll down the sidewalk and visit the other stores."

Julie walked to one dirty window and looked up and down the street. "Someone has done a lot of work out there. Was that you?"

"A lot of local people pitched in to help. I mostly provided the funds. The people who grew up in this town are committed to bringing it back to life. So am I."

"This is a far cry from Manhattan."

So, she'd done her homework. "It is, and that's what I love about it."

She nodded and looked back out the

window. "I'd want to brew some micro batches on site. Would I have any trouble with doing that?"

"Trouble?"

"Zoning. Licenses?"

"No problem on the zoning. I've already spoken to the city planner about that and been assured they won't stand in the way of any business that wants to claim this corner as their own. As for a liquor license, that would be up to you to acquire."

"Can I see the rest of the place?"

An hour later, they sat across from each other at the new diner out on the highway. Scott would have preferred someplace quieter, but Julie insisted. When they were through talking, she was heading to Dallas to pick up some supplies and could just hop on the freeway from there.

Julie pushed plates out of the way, making room for the pad of paper she had brought along to take notes on. "Look." She scribbled furiously, drawing a rough sketch of the main floor of the building. "See? There needs to be a bar here. Then over here"—she drew more lines—"there needs to be tables, maybe long ones, picnic style."

"Here. Let me show you what I had in mind." He swung the pad to his side of the table. She handed over her pen, and he drew another rough sketch. Before he finished, Julie slid in beside him and grabbed the pen from his hand.

"No." She shook her head. "I see what you're getting at, but that won't work."

Scott surrendered the pad. She tore off the top sheet and began sketching on a new page.

"This is the tasting room, right? So the bar has to be here because that's the only place we would have access to the keg storage area."

"What if we did this?" Scott hunched over the pad to draw his latest idea.

Wanting to see better, Julie ducked her head so their faces were only inches apart. Scott scooted over to make room for the leggy blonde. In the short time he'd known her, he'd come to the conclusion that the dumb blonde jokes didn't pertain to her. She was smart and beautiful. If he hadn't given his heart to another, he'd find her earthy scent and coltish figure attractive. But he had given his heart, and though he noticed Julie's qualities, he just wasn't interested, and as far as he could tell, her only interest in him had to do with the property he owned, which made working with her easier. Heads together, they worked for the better part of an hour, drawing, revising, and troubleshooting before reaching a tentative agreement on the layout of the key elements of the design.

"Can you do that?" she asked.

"I'll talk to my restoration expert and see. If it can be done, do we have a deal?"

"I'll want my attorney to look over the paperwork before I sign anything, but yeah, I think we have a deal." Her smile nearly blinded him. She placed a hand on his forearm then before he could stop her, she leaned in and kissed him on the cheek. "I've got to go."

She tore the top few sheets off the notepad, left them on the table. Faster than a dust devil, she packed up her stuff, leaving him sitting there with a pile of crude design notes and the bill.

~ ~ ~

Roseanne was starving—something she was all too familiar with these days. Seems she was either sick at her stomach or hungry. This was a hungry day. She'd stayed up too late the night before then slept in this morning, causing her to have to rush to get to her doctor's appointment in Prairieview. There'd been no time for breakfast. She'd had to wait nearly an hour to see the doctor who rushed in after delivering a baby at the hospital across the street. It was a good excuse but hadn't done Roseanne's stomach any good.

The billboard advertising fresh pastries at the next exit made her mouth water. Taking the next exit, she pulled into the parking lot for the flashy new diner. She grabbed her wallet and went inside. Next to the cashier, a glass case containing all manner of delectable goodies caught her attention. She spent a minute scanning the contents, deciding which one, or two, to take home with her.

Her gaze locked on the thick chocolate brownie topped with chopped nuts. "I'll take two of those, please."

While the cashier bagged her selection, Roseanne checked out the dining room. Not too many locals came this far out to grab a bite to eat, but a few did. Her gaze skimmed over the crowd, stopping on one head in particular. Scott Ramsey sat in a booth about halfway back along the front wall, his back to the door, his head bent as if carrying on a private conversation with the blonde next to him.

Brownies forgotten, Roseanne stared at the couple. They sure looked cozy, sharing the same side of the booth, practically breathing the same air. She inhaled deep, willing her stomach to ease, remembering what it had been like to breathe the rarified air around Scott Ramsey. It had been weeks since she'd seen him, but she knew firsthand how he could draw you in, make you feel like you were the only woman in the world. Even with all the food smells permeating the air, her nostrils knew his scent. Knew the heat that radiated off him.

"That will be five dollars and thirty-one cents."

"Oh. Sorry." Roseanne fumbled with her wallet. She handed over a ten dollar bill, her gaze wandering back to the couple in the booth while the clerk counted out her change. Suddenly, the couple sat up and began talking. In profile, she could see it was a friendly conversation, animated and pleasant. The woman leaned in and placed a cutesy kiss on Scott's cheek, stunning Roseanne with its familiarity. How many times had she pecked him on the cheek when they parted company? Too many to count.

"Your change, miss."

Roseanne jerked her attention to the young man behind the counter. "Yes. Thank you."

She took the change, stuffing it absently in her pants pocket. She grabbed the white pastry bag, planning to make her escape before Scott or his mystery woman saw her. Without checking to see if either one had left the booth, Roseanne made a dash for the door and her car. She'd just put the vehicle in gear when the diner door opened again and the blonde stepped out. Head down, she dug in her purse for her keys. Roseanne knew her. Had done business with her.

Julie Davis. She truly was a Lucky Lady.

~ ~ ~

It had been two weeks since she'd seen Scott having an early lunch—or was it a late breakfast?—with Julie Davis, and she refused to think about it. Much. In fact, she'd relegated herself to only thinking about her baby's daddy with another woman three times a day—morning, noon, and night.

Her thoughts weren't rational. She knew they weren't, but she couldn't stop them. She'd tried, immersing herself in work. The garden hadn't been this weed-free in years, the closets had never been cleaner, and the woodwork had never been shinier. Kay had scolded her more than once for doing the job she'd hired

Maria to do, but Roseanne couldn't sit still.

So, when it came, she welcomed the call from Randy Tucker. Showing her beloved home to his carpenter and designer gave her something to do besides dwell on the fact that she really, truly, was going to be a single mother. She'd finally admitted to herself that in the back of her mind she'd hoped Scott would come begging for her forgiveness. Having met his parents at Becky's wedding, she had a better understanding of why he hadn't asked her to go to their anniversary party. Talk about a piece of work. If Scott hadn't been the spitting image of his father, she'd swear he had been adopted.

But that didn't excuse his behavior. He should have told her about the party. Let her decide if she wanted to go or not, but the fact that he hadn't invited her to a family event proved how little their relationship meant to him. Since she'd booted him out of her house, he hadn't made a single attempt to talk to her, other than at the wedding, when he'd had no choice.

She could still feel his arousal pressed against her backside, feel his breath on her neck, hear the desire in his voice as he held her close while the photographer snapped photo after photo of the happy couple and their entourage. *He didn't have to proposition you.* She'd practically dragged him back to her bedroom. That was true, but knowing he still found her desirable didn't mean squat. He'd already found someone else to have lunch or, gag, breakfast with. Just went to prove women were a dime a dozen in his eyes.

The bell on the front door jingled. *Right on time.* Roseanne joined Kay in the foyer to welcome their guests.

"Mr. Tucker," she said, offering her hand. "I didn't know you were going to be here, too."

Taking her hand, his eyes appraised her with a warmth she hadn't felt in a long time. "Couldn't resist another chance to look at a lovely lady."

Roseanne wasn't sure if he was talking about the house or her. She smiled and nodded. Randy Tucker was handsome, and his manners were impeccable. As a woman, she could appreciate those qualities, but she simply wasn't interested. She'd already made one bad choice, and getting involved with Tucker while she carried another man's child would be idiotic. She gently took her hand away, silently offering an apology for not reciprocating his interest. Maybe in a few years, when the wound wasn't so fresh, she'd consider dating again. Find some nice guy who could love her and her kid.

Pipe dream. That's what that is.

"As it turns out, something has come up," she lied. "I've asked Kay to show you around. She knows almost as much about the house as I do." Another lie, but she wasn't the least bit sorry. Ever since she'd seen Scott with Julie Davis, she'd felt as if she were on a sinking ship. It was time she focused on survival, and that meant delegating the less important duties to others. This was one of them.

Kay stepped forward. "Welcome to The Yellow Rose. If you'll follow me?

We'll begin the tour in the kitchen. I have a pitcher of sweet tea and a plate of scones, if anyone is interested."

The group filed past, Tucker staying behind. "I meant what I said. I came to see a lovely lady. It's a darned shame she's busy. Maybe we could have dinner instead?"

Roseanne clenched her hands into fists and searched the floor for a polite way to say no.

"Just dinner. No expectations, just conversation and some food you don't have to cook. I'd love to pick your brain about the restoration I'm doing downtown."

She shook her head. "The offer is tempting, but no. I…can't."

He dipped his chin. "I see. Well, if you change your mind, you have my number."

"I do. Thanks for understanding."

"Guess I better get in there before all the scones are gone, then."

Roseanne laughed. "Yes, you'd better."

She watched him go then returned to

her office, shutting the door behind her. She had a few things to go over before she met later that day with the attorney she'd engaged to look into her rights as a single parent.

PART THREE
"You may all go to hell, and I will go to Texas."
Davy Crockett

CHAPTER TWENTY

Roseanne rushed into her best friend's office, skidding to a stop in front of her desk. "Becky! Guess who I just got off the phone with?"

Becky Adams sat back in her chair and smiled. "Don't know, but I bet you're going to tell me."

"An agent! She called me out of the blue. Said I queried a friend of hers who no longer handles nonfiction, and she passed my letter on to her."

"That's great, I guess. What did she say?"

"She wants to represent me!" She couldn't help it. She squealed. "She said she'd send a contract, and that I should have an attorney look it over. Oh my God. I can't believe an agent actually called me!"

Becky laughed. "I told you someone would, didn't I?"

"You did, but I didn't believe you." Running out of steam, she finally sat, clasping on the edge of Becky's desk to ground her. "Who would want to represent little ole me? It's amazing."

"Not so much amazing as exciting. What else did she say?"

"Oh, Lord." She closed her eyes and tried to recall the entire conversation, but parts of it were lost to her. She'd been too keyed up to grasp it all. "She said she'd seen the sample chapter I sent and loved it. She said everyone loves a bed-and-breakfast, and who wouldn't want to make those scrumptious meals for their family or guests." Her eyes popped open. "And she said she knows two publishers who have been looking for just this sort of project." Roseanne forced her hands to her lap. "Is that cool, or what?"

"It's super cool," Becky confirmed. "I knew you could do it. You can say I told you so anytime now."

"Okay. Okay. You told me so, smarty pants."

"What's next?"

"I need to find a lawyer to look at the contract. She said she'd email me a copy then overnight the print version." She dug her phone out of her pocket to check her email. "It's here! Oh my God. I can't believe it. This is really happening."

"We have a lawyer we use to handle all of our contracts. I could ask him to take a look, if you want."

"Wow. Yes, that would be great."

Becky picked up the handset on her desk phone. "Email me that file and I'll print it out for him."

Roseanne forwarded the email while her best friend talked to the lawyer. When Becky ended the call, she opened the email, and, in a few seconds, the printer behind her desk began to whir. It wasn't long before it spit out several sheets of paper. Becky scooped them up, smacked the stapler head to hold them all together, and passed them over the desk.

"Here you go. You know where the

new offices are, don't you? Take the long hallway that goes off to the left when you go in the studio building."

"I remember. The conference room is down that hall, too."

"That's the one. His name is Pete Shannon. His office is about halfway down, before you get to the conference room."

"I can't thank you enough, Becks. You're the best friend ever."

"Have you thought any more about the other big thing in your life?"

Roseanne sobered. "Every minute of every day. But you already know that. What you really want to know is if I'm going to tell him anytime soon."

"You know I think you should."

"He's moved on, Becks."

She leaned forward, crossing her arms on the top of the desk. A deep crease formed between her eyebrows. "What are you talking about?"

"I saw him with a woman. They looked awfully cozy, and it was the middle of the day." She got up and shut the office door. The only other office at this end of the hallway was Ford's, and he usually worked with headphones on, but you never knew when someone would drop by. Becky kept an open-door policy with her employees.

"Spill, girlfriend." Becky was all ears as Roseanne told her about seeing Scott and Julie Davis at the diner out on the interstate.

"I don't believe it," Becks said.

"I saw it with my own eyes. I bet he's working his way through every single woman in town. Maybe some of the married ones, too."

Becky sat back in her chair again. "I'm sorry, Roseanne. Ford said he was a good guy, and I took his word for it."

"Not your fault. I knew he was a damned Yankee, but I still fell for his charm. Just my luck to get knocked up in the process."

"Do you want me to talk to Ford? If he knew, he wouldn't let Scott get away without at least paying child support."

Roseanne shook her head. "No, please don't say anything to anyone. I've consulted an attorney. He says I need to tell Scott eventually." She sighed. "Truthfully? I don't want his money. If he can't be a hands-on father to his child, then I don't want anything else he has to offer."

"Okay." Becky sounded skeptical. "But put me on record as objecting to this plan of action. The baby is just as much his responsibility as it yours."

Roseanne waved the papers in her hand. "I should take these over, see what your lawyer has to say. If this agent can sell the book to a publisher, and she says she can, maybe I'll have the means to support the baby myself. Then I really can tell Scott Ramsey where he can go."

~ ~ ~

"What do you think?" Scott and Ford had just completed a walk-through of the newly completed office space that the company they had founded together in New York would now occupy on Main Street in Butte Plains.

"It's fantastic." Ford ran a hand down the original molding surrounding the front door of the century-and-a-half-old building. "Makes me want to renovate my office at the plant."

"Why would you want to get rid of the institutional green paint and the layers of dust? It would destroy the character of the place." Scott chuckled at his own joke.

"Seriously? Right? Besides, I think the dust is all that's holding the place together," Ford said, laughing along with his friend. He sobered. "Becky gave me a new desk chair for my birthday. I love it, and I know her heart was in the right place, but it doesn't go with the desk, or anything else in the room."

"Nothing goes with anything in that office. Face it, Ford, every Adams for the last hundred years has left his mark on that room. Maybe it's time you left yours."

Ford nodded. "Maybe it is." He looked around at the beautifully restored building, taking in all the details. "You know, the original office was in the building we turned into studio space. My great-grandfather built the current building and moved his office there. We've got two factories going now, a distribution center, a television studio, and we're thinking of opening a retail outlet on a piece of land out by the highway. It would be nice to consolidate all the corporate structure in one place."

"Have you seen the buildings over on the next block? I bet you could pick up the entire block for a song. Lots of square footage."

"Can I afford it?"

"Shut the fuck up. It's an investment in the future of Adams Manufacturing and Butte Plains."

"You sound just like the mayor."

"You mean the part-time mayor slash Realtor."

"Yeah. Him." Ford, hands on his hips, took one last look at the new space. "Okay. Let's go take a look."

They stopped on the corner. Ford pointed to the windows blanked out with brown paper. "What's going in there?"

"Lucky Lady Brewery's new tasting room." The light changed, and they crossed the street.

"Wow. How did you make that happen? I hear the owner is a recluse."

"Her name's Julie Davis. I don't know

that she's a recluse, just a workaholic. Runs that entire microbrewery all by herself. We've finally come to terms on the lease. Waiting for the Historical Society to agree to the interior restoration. Once they do that, and the city issues permits, we'll get started on the project."

"Using the same company?"

"Yeah. Tucker Restoration out of Dallas. They did a great job on our office space, and you should see how the house is coming along. It's costing a fortune, but it's worth every penny to see the place come alive again."

They stopped at the next corner, looking south down Elm Street.

"The whole block is empty?" Ford asked.

"Yep. I looked at it when I was thinking about buying downtown. Would have bought it, but I figured the most bang for my buck was on Main. However, you don't need that kind of exposure. A block over from the action would be perfect for your corporate headquarters. There are still a couple of storefronts available on

Main. You could open a factory outlet store downtown."

"It would be good to have a way to get rid of manufacturing overruns." Ford crossed the street to get a good look at the abandoned buildings. "This could work for our offices. What about parking?"

Scott led Ford to the end of the block to a large, vacant lot piled with old tires and derelict appliances. "Parking garage, right here."

"Think the city would let me build a parking structure here?"

"I think they'd let you build anything you want as long as you clean the place up. It's an eyesore. Throw in some free parking on the ground level for tourists and shoppers, and they'll probably pitch in the building permits for free."

"It's something to think about, for sure. Let me run it by Becky. She knows more about our financial situation than I do, but I think she'll go for the idea. She hates our current situation."

"I've gotten to know the folks in City Hall pretty well. If you decide to do this, let me know, and I'll see if I can get some concessions for you."

Ford laughed and shook his head. "Look at you. All chummy with City Hall. You probably know more about real estate in this town than the Realtors. You've really settled in here, haven't you?"

"I guess I have." He kicked at a pebble on the sidewalk, sent it skittering into the street. "My apartment in New York sold last week. Made a shit-ton of money on it." He lifted his chin toward the empty block of buildings. "If you don't want to buy it, I will. Lease it back to you, renovated of course, for a dollar a month or something. If you want to buy somewhere down the road, I'd make you a good deal on it."

Ford whistled low. "That's a deal I don't think we can pass up. Let me talk to Becky."

"Sounds good. Seriously, I'm okay either way. These buildings are fabulous. They deserve to be saved."

CHAPTER TWENTY-ONE

They walked back to the new offices of Ramsey and Adams Design and Engineering where they'd left their cars. Scott waved good-bye to his friend. Alone, he opened the door to the empty storefront two doors down. Bouncing his keys in his hand, he let his eyes adjust to the dim light coming in the dirty windows and tried to envision the space in another way.

He wondered if Roseanne remembered telling him about her idea. It was a lazy Sunday. The weekend guests had checked out, and the bed-and-breakfast was empty except for them. They'd spent the afternoon in bed, making love slow, lingering afterward to cuddle and talk. He'd listened to her dreams for the future, tucking them away to examine later when her body wasn't there to distract him.

"This will do," he said to the empty room. It had been a hotel in another life. The commercial kitchen in the back was a relic, but that could be replaced easily enough. He stood in the center of the front room, imagining the way she'd set it up. A few tables here in the front room so people strolling along the sidewalk could see inside. The old guest rooms upstairs restored and converted to dining rooms.

A tea room. High tea in the afternoons, just tea and pastries the rest of the day. Roseanne's baked goods were to die for.

The back would be Roseanne's personal domain. Her test kitchen. No more grabbing a few hours each day in the kitchen at the B&B to work on her recipes. She could experiment all she wanted and hire others to prepare and serve the tea menu.

It would fit perfectly into the backdrop

of downtown and, with the aid of the other businesses moving in, would have a steady clientele.

He'd already hired a PR firm to promote Butte Plains as a weekend destination. With the new airstrip, they were promoting the town to private plane owners' groups. Who knew there were flying clubs out there had fly-in meetings? The PR people were working with the new hotel by the freeway and Roseanne's bed-and-breakfast to provide a group rate for certain holiday weekends to encourage the clubs to visit. Ads were being placed in travel magazines across the country, but primarily in the South and Southwest.

He locked up and headed to his car. He had a golf course in need of a new owner to check out.

~ ~ ~

It was happening. It was *really* happening!

For once, Roseanne's stomach was queasy for another reason besides being pregnant.

"Are you packed yet?" Becky called

from the hallway. "It's time to go."

"Done." Stuffing one last-minute item into her suitcase, she closed the lid and zipped up the case she'd borrowed from her best friend.

"We've got to go, girlfriend. You've got dinner reservations tonight. Don't want to be late." Becky stood in the doorway to Roseanne's third-floor room.

Roseanne sat on the bed next to her borrowed suitcase. "Please come with me tonight. I'm begging you. My agent said it would be okay."

"Nope. I'm going to order room service then enjoy the hell out of an expensive bottle of wine and that gorgeous soaking tub in our suite. Besides, you don't need me. Your agent and your editor will be there, fawning over you like you're some kind of big shot, which you are. This is your deal. You worked hard for it, so enjoy. Besides, after my meeting tomorrow morning, the two of us are going to celebrate in style."

"Okay, okay." She stood and slid the luggage to the floor.

"Leave that," Becky said. She leaned

out the door and yelled, "Ford! Come get Roseanne's suitcase."

Loud footsteps sounded on the back stairs.

"I can—"

"Nonsense. Ford can carry it down twice as fast as either of us could."

"You haven't told him, have you?"

Becky swiped her finger across her chest twice. "Cross my heart." She gave her friend the evil eye. "But I'm going to if you don't tell you-know-who soon."

"Tell who what?" Ford asked, huffing from climbing all the way to the top floor.

"Nothing," Roseanne and Becky said in unison.

Ford reached for the handle on the luggage. "Got it. None of my business." He disappeared, case in hand. The women shared a look they'd perfected over years of friendship. The discussion wasn't over, just tabled until they were alone and had plenty of time.

"Let's get this show on the road before I chicken out." Roseanne headed for the door, Becky on her heels.

Roseanne had only traveled in such

luxury one other time—when she'd flown with Scott in one of the Ramsey family jets to Las Vegas. The one Ford had chartered for his wife and her best friend for this trip to New York City wasn't quite as elaborate on the inside, but it came close. Before they left the ground, the flight attendant offered them an array of drinks. Becky chose champagne while Roseanne opted for fizzy water in a pretty bottle.

"I don't know how I can thank you and Ford enough for doing this for me."

"No thanks needed. This is a business trip for me, too. I've needed to meet with these people forever, but Ford didn't want me to go alone, and, with everything we've got going on right now, one of us needs to be in the office. You couldn't have sold your cookbook at a better time for us." She lifted her champagne flute. "I thank you for that from the bottom of my heart."

Roseanne raised her water bottle in salute. "The fact that you're getting a whole weekend in a luxury suite in New York has absolutely nothing to do with your enthusiasm for this trip, I suppose."

"Not a damned thing, sister."

Takeoff went smoothly, and soon they were at cruising altitude. Roseanne reclined her seat and tried to enjoy the moment. She couldn't believe how much her life had changed since that trip to Las Vegas. She'd ended her relationship with Scott only to find out days later she was pregnant. By all appearances he'd moved on—she'd seen the evidence with her own eyes. So even if she did want him back, that was out of the question. Almost paralyzed by the daunting task ahead of her, she'd still managed to orchestrate Becky and Ford's wedding. Then, the calls had come that made all the difference. First, an agent then the call that she'd sold Roseanne's first cookbook to an editor at a major publishing house in New York. The advance they were offering wasn't enormous, but substantial, her agent called it.

At any rate, the money would allow Roseanne to rent a small place of her own where she'd have room to raise her child. This trip was so she could meet her new editor and discuss their marketing and book launch plans. She got butterflies in her stomach every time she thought about it. Or was that the baby moving around?

She placed her hand on her belly which was now gently rounded. Easy to hide still, if she wore the right clothes, but not for much longer.

"You know you're going to have to tell him, don't you?"

"I know." Roseanne sighed. She should have known Becky wouldn't let the subject drop. "I will. I've put it off because my lawyer suggested I draw up a custody agreement to present to Scott when I tell him. Be proactive. Until I sold this book, I didn't have the money to pay him to prepare the papers. I'll have him get started on it as soon as I get home."

"I know you were counting on Scott going back home, but, from what Ford says, he isn't going to do that. He wants to stay in Butte Plains."

Roseanne huffed and stared out the window. "I bet he'll run far and fast as soon as he finds out he's going to be a father. No way will he stick around for that."

"I don't know. I sort of think you need to give him the benefit of the doubt."

Roseanne shot her a look. "Seriously?"

"Yeah, I'm serious. You met his parents at our wedding. They're nothing like him. I can believe he was protecting you when he didn't take you to their party."

"Maybe he thought he was protecting me, but that still doesn't account for him not telling me about the party and letting me decide."

"Turns out the decision was made for you anyway, and not by Scott, but by Scott's baby. Talk all you want about not being allowed to make your own decisions, but remember you aren't giving him any choices, either."

"I know." She wasn't being fair to Scott, but every time she thought about telling him, legal papers in hand or not, her stomach rebelled. What if he stayed in Butte Plains because of the child?

What if he married someone else and had more kids? God, she'd have to live in the same town with him the rest of her life—see his other kids grow up with a full-time father. How would she ever explain that to her child? She closed her eyes and searched deep for strength. "I'll tell him, Becks. I swear I will."

~ ~ ~

The car and driver Ford had hired to cart them around town met them at the airport. Roseanne had thought it was even more excess, but as soon as she saw the traffic and crowded sidewalks, she changed her mind.

"How does anyone ever get anywhere in this city?" she asked.

"Don't know," Becky said, tipping her head to get a better look at a building. "Ford had a house in Westchester and rarely went into the city. I can see why."

"Me, too." She'd never seen so many people in one place, and all of them appeared to be in a hurry to get somewhere else. "Where do you think all these people are going?"

"I have no idea. Work? School?

Shopping? All those things we use our cars for."

Roseanne shook her head. "It's crazy. I don't know how they stand it. I like my space." At a stoplight, she saw a woman pushing a stroller across the busy intersection. Mother? Nanny? Instantly, she thought about the child she carried. What if Scott won custody? Somewhere amid all these buildings that blocked the sun was the place he called home. Would he want to bring the baby here to raise? Would he hire a stranger to look after their child while he darted around the city, racing to nowhere? Her hand went to her belly, seeking comfort for herself and silently reassuring the child within.

"Are you okay?" Becky placed a hand on Roseanne's arm. "Is the baby alright?"

"I'm fine. We're fine," she corrected.

"You looked like you were in pain."

She shook her head. "No. I was just thinking. If Scott sues for custody and wins, he'd probably want to bring the baby here. People like him don't raise kids. They hire nannies to do that for them. I can't let that happen."

"First, I don't think you have anything to worry about. Scott seems like a reasonable person. Besides, we're talking about Texas. What judge would let a single dad take a child away from its mother and haul off halfway across the country with it?" She shook her head so hard her ponytail slapped against her cheeks. "Not going to happen. But," she said, "kids are resilient. They adapt to their surroundings. I'm certain there are plenty of happy, healthy children growing up here."

"Ugh. That's not what I wanted to hear."

"I know it's not, but I think you're projecting sins on Scott without any grounds. You won't know what his intentions are until you tell him about the baby."

Roseanne shot her friend a warning look.

"Okay. I'll shut up. But you know I'm right."

They passed a glass-faced tower that seemed to have no pinnacle. So cold and impersonal, reflecting, deflecting.

Windows with no soul. Roseanne wiped a tear from her eye. She couldn't wait to complete her business and get back home.

CHAPTER TWENTY-TWO

Roseanne followed the maître d' as he threaded his way through the crowded restaurant to a small room on the second floor. Her dinner companions were already there. They stood and introduced themselves.

"Roseanne, I'm so happy to meet you. I'm Liz Rothstein."

This was the agent she'd spoken to several times on the phone. Roseanne smiled and extended her hand to the woman who might have been five feet tall, weighing in at maybe a hundred pounds with a halo of dark, frizzy hair that framed her narrow face. She had a booming voice that made her seem larger than she actually was. "It's nice to meet you, Liz."

"And this is your editor, Paula Ramone." She indicated the other woman at the table. The two women couldn't have been more different. Paula towered over the diminutive agent and, thanks to her generous curves, probably outweighed her by fifty pounds. She'd pulled her straight, glossy black hair to one side, holding it in place with a jeweled clip.

"Hello, Roseanne. It's nice to meet you."

The two shook hands. "My pleasure," Roseanne said, taking the seat across from the two women. She grabbed the neatly folded napkin at her place setting, spreading it across her lap to give herself a moment to calm down. She'd had all of ten minutes to enjoy their hotel room before she'd returned to the car for another hair-raising trip through man-made canyons filled with cars and people.

"How was your trip?" Paula asked.

"Uneventful. Which is exactly what

you hope a plane ride will be, right?"

The women laughed. "True," Liz said. They exchanged polite conversation while waiters in white coats and black slacks bustled around them, bringing baskets of bread and dishes of fragrant olive oil seasoned with cracked pepper.

"I hope you like Italian," Paula said. "This is one of the best places in the city to get authentic Italian food."

"She should know," Liz said.

"Italian, through and through," Paula confirmed. "But that doesn't mean I can't enjoy other types of food. As a matter of fact, I'm a food junkie. Your recipes really caught my eye, Roseanne. And the concept is something I think every hostess can relate to whether you have guests you want to pamper or just want to do something special for your family."

"Thank you. We try to pamper our guests at the bed-and-breakfast. If they wanted a cold, impersonal experience, they'd stay at a chain hotel. They choose The Yellow Rose because they want more."

"Exactly!" Liz said. "Plus, your recipes

aren't so complicated that it takes a trained chef to prepare them."

"I've found that complicated doesn't always mean better."

Waiters appeared with platters of steaming dishes they placed in the middle of the table for everyone to serve themselves. "Like Italian food. A few key ingredients and you have a simple, but delicious meal. Help yourself." Paula pointed to each dish, naming them as she went. Roseanne's mouth watered.

"It all looks delicious." She ladled a generous helping of spaghetti with meat sauce onto her plate, topping it off with a slice of garlic bread.

"Wine?" Paula lifted the bottle that had been opened and left on the table to "breathe."

"No, thank you. I think I'll stick with water."

"Liz?"

"Sure." She held her glass while Paula poured.

"You sure?" Paula asked again.

Roseanne waved her offer away. "Positive. But, thank you."

They focused on filling their stomachs for a few minutes, breaking the silence with the occasional comment about the food which was delicious. Roseanne hadn't experimented much with Italian dishes, but she vowed to give it a try when she got home. She especially loved the array of desserts that arrived as they were taking their last bites.

"Oh, yum!" She wiped a glob of sweet cheese filling from the corner of her mouth. "This is fabulous."

"Cannoli is my favorite," Paula confessed. "I could eat my weight in them, which is saying something." She laughed and reached for her second one.

With the help of her dinner companions, Roseanne tasted all the confections and felt ready to burst when the waiters came to clear the table. "You know I'm going to go home and try to recreate everything I've eaten here."

"I can send you some of my family recipes if you want."

"I want." Roseanne beamed. Family recipes were the best. "Most of the recipes in my book are adaptations of my grandmother's recipes. She was a fabulous cook, but ingredients have changed over the years. There are healthier options and, in some cases, more flavorful ones."

"Which brings us back to business," Paula said. "Normally, something like this would take years to get out, but we've had some setbacks with one of our usually reliable authors. That's bad for us, but great for you. We want to fast-track your book—get it out in time for the holidays."

"I don't know what to say. This is—"

"A big, freakin' deal," Paula said. "I've already sent the recipes to an independent test kitchen we use. They'll work up all the crap no one wants to know about their food—calorie count, fat, and salt numbers. The art department has been working overtime on a cover. I have some ideas to show you, see what you think."

Roseanne's head swam. Everything came at her too fast for her to keep up.

Paula continued on, oblivious to Roseanne's state of mind. "We'll launch big with some cooking shows. I've got contacts at the Food Network, so that shouldn't be a problem. I'm positive I can get you a spot on all the major morning shows. Then we'll hit all the major markets, New York, Chicago, Dallas, Los Angeles. Their local morning shows followed up by signings at the large retailers. If we have time, I'd like to squeeze in some signings in the satellite cities, too."

Satellite cities? What the hell are those? Television appearances and book signings all over the country? What had she signed on for?

"Oh, and my people, *your* people, are working on some magazine interviews, too. What do you think? Sound good?"

Roseanne knew she must be staring like a loon, but she couldn't find words.

"That's an ambitious plan," Liz said. "Are you sure you can pull it off in time for the holidays?"

"It's going to be a tall order, but yes, I think we can."

"I can't do it."

"What?" Both women screeched at

the same time.

"I said, I can't do it. Maybe some of it, but not all."

"Why not? Do you understand what kind of opportunity this is? This is the kind of marketing package usually reserved for top-tier authors. We're doing you a favor. A big favor." Paula's tone had reached the same temperature as the ice in Roseanne's water glass, and sounded just as brittle.

Roseanne twisted her hands in her lap. She'd never imagined something like this happening.

"Roseanne." Liz reached across the table. "Are you okay?"

"I'm...fine." She took a deep breath then let it out. "I appreciate the opportunity, but I can't do that kind of tour."

"Why?" Liz's normally booming voice held nothing but concern now. "Tell us why."

"Because I'm pregnant." A glass shattered somewhere behind her. Roseanne ignored the commotion and continued. "The baby is due around

Christmas."

Both women stared at her, their mouths open in shock.

"I'm sorry. I would have told you, but it…. I didn't—"

"How could you have known?" Liz said. She turned to Paula. "What can you do?"

"I don't know. I'll have to go back to the team and see what we can salvage from this." She made no attempt to hide her disappointment. "I wish I'd known."

Roseanne opened her mouth to apologize again, but Liz cut her off. "There's no way she could have known you would do something like this. You should have told me. I could have told her, and then we wouldn't be in this mess."

"Liz said it would be next year before the book came out, at the earliest."

"That's the normal timeline, yes," Paula said.

"This isn't her fault."

"No, I suppose it isn't." Paula signaled for the waiter. When he arrived, she asked for the check. They sat in silence until the back and forth was done and the bill paid. Paula stood. "It really is a pleasure to have met you, Roseanne." She turned to the agent. "Liz. I'll be in touch."

"I'm so sorry."

"Don't be. Like I told Paula…this isn't your fault. She knows better than to do something like this without checking with the author first. The contract is signed. If they want to launch on an accelerated timeline, that's their business, but you are under no obligation to participate in the tour."

"My contract says that?"

"It has an out for extenuating circumstances. I'm sure your attorney noted that clause."

Roseanne nodded. "Yes. He mentioned that, but—"

"I know. Don't worry about it. She'll fume about it for a day or two then she'll revise the schedule. If she insists on the early release date, then we'll agree to a fair amount of promotional appearances. You can do the morning show interviews from home via satellite link. Surely there's a television station near you?"

"As a matter of fact, my best friend and her husband produce their own home shopping show. They recently launched a new network. Maybe you've heard of it—The Adult Shopping Network?"

"Who hasn't heard of it? They call him The Backdoor Billionaire, right?"

"Yes. His name is Ford Adams. He married my best friend, Becky Jean Parker. They have a state-of-the-art studio, and I think they have satellite access. It's just a few blocks from my house."

"That's perfect! I'll email Paula and give her that information. You could even pre-tape interviews for some of the smaller markets, and I'll do my best to keep the personal appearances confined to a decent geographical range to minimize travel. Would that work for you?"

"I think I could handle that." She'd have no choice but to tell Scott about the baby if she was going to be on television unless she could convince them to do tight, headshots only.

"Then it's settled. I'll have a talk with Paula, get this straightened out. Don't worry."

CHAPTER TWENTY-THREE

It had been a week since her trip to New York, and she hadn't heard a thing from her editor or her agent. She tried not to think about it. No news was good news, right? When she'd returned to the hotel and told Becky what had happened, she'd insisted on calling the attorney who had looked over the contract for Roseanne. He'd confirmed that yes, she had agreed to make personal appearances and participate in marketing the book, but that in no way obligated her to do anything that would be detrimental to her health or well-being. In his opinion, asking a woman in the last weeks of her pregnancy to traipse around the country to sell a book fell under the "asking too much" umbrella, especially since the timeline Roseanne had agreed to had been changed on her without notice.

The confirmation made her feel better about the whole thing, but she was still afraid they'd find some way to weasel out of the contract based on her inability to fulfill her end of the marketing plan. When Kay knocked on her office door, she welcomed the interruption. Anything to keep her mind occupied so she didn't dwell on things she couldn't control.

"What is it, Kay?"

"There's a gentleman here to see you. He said it was personal."

"Who is it?"

Kay shrugged. "No idea. He's not from around here, I can tell you that. Too slick. Lawyer would be my guess."

Roseanne's heart sank. Her worst fears had come true. They'd found a way to break the contract. She opened the top drawer of her desk to grab a tissue from the box she kept there, giving herself a moment to fight back the tears. She could be a watering pot later. Right now, she needed to be strong, assertive. Her attorney had assured her they couldn't use her pregnancy as a reason to nullify the contract. "Would you show him to my office, please?" She'd meet him on her own turf where she held the position of authority.

"Yes, ma'am. I'd be just as happy to show him the door."

Out of necessity, she'd told Kay about her pregnancy. The woman hadn't been surprised. She'd seen Roseanne's battle with morning sickness and fatigue, and lately she'd noticed her expanding belly. Always loyal, she'd become Roseanne's protector, taking on more responsibility and putting in more hours.

Roseanne smiled. "I appreciate the offer, but he'd only come back another time. Best hear what he has to say so I can deal with it."

"If you say so."

"I say so. Show him in."

She quickly dabbed the extra moisture from the corners of her eyes and ran a hand over her hair, smoothing an errant strand back in place. Whatever he had to say, she'd hear him out then call her attorney and fill him in. Together, they'd come up with a plan to respond.

Kay appeared in the hallway, followed by a man wearing a three-piece suit and carrying a briefcase that screamed expensive lawyer.

"I'll be in the kitchen, Ms. Meadows. If you need anything, just holler." The way she emphasized the word anything brought a smile to Roseanne's lips. All she'd have to do was raise her voice, and Kay would come running, rolling pin in hand, most likely.

Remaining seated, she said, "Thank you, Kay." She shifted her gaze to her visitor. "I'm Roseanne Meadows. You wanted to see me?"

He stepped inside. "My name is Roland Meiser." He slid a card from an inside pocket of his suit jacket and handed it to her. "Senior partner at Meiser, Swift and Harding in New York City."

Roseanne took the card, glancing briefly at it before dropping it on top of the stack of purchase orders she'd been sorting before he arrived. "What's this about, Mr. Meiser?"

He swung his briefcase into his lap and opened it. "I'm here to make you an offer."

What? "I don't understand. An offer? From whom?"

"I represent the concerns of the Ramsey family." He held out a sheaf of papers. Roseanne made no attempt to take them.

Her blood ran cold. "Again. What is this about?"

He dropped the papers on her desk and stood. "You have forty-eight hours to respond before the offer is off the table for good."

"And if I refuse this offer?"

"Then my client has instructed me to file for sole custody of the child you carry. You will never see your child, Ms. Meadows. My client has the means and the clout to have the child removed from your care the moment it takes its first breath. Don't make the mistake of thinking you can fight us on this. You will lose. Take the offer, Ms. Meadows." He stopped in the doorframe and turned. "I look forward to hearing from you soon."

She couldn't speak. Couldn't breathe. Couldn't move. Her gaze landed on the stack of papers he'd left on her desk. The Ramsey's. Scott. It was too much to process. If she didn't take the offer. What offer? Reaching out as if afraid the paper might strike at any moment, she dragged them forward. Slowly, she forced her fingers to function, lifting the papers from the desk. It took a moment for her vision to clear enough for her to make out the neatly typed words.

She read. Then read again. Words with no meaning floated before her eyes. Settlement. Paternity. Cease and desist. Forbidden. Claim.

No. No. "Noooo!"

"Roseanne! What's the matter? Is it the baby?"

Kay. Sweet Kay holding her. "I've got to go."

"No, no you don't. Everything's going to be alright. Should I call the doctor?"

Doctor? "No. I've got to go. See that

bastard.”

“Who? The doctor?”

“No. I’ve got to go.” She stood, forcing Kay to step back.

“I’ll drive you. Let me get my purse.” When Kay returned, Roseanne held the papers in her fist, her only tether to reality. “Where are we going?”

“I don’t know. Where he is.” Where would he be? She didn’t have a clue where he spent his days. “The leather factory?”

“I know where that is. My cousin used to work there.”

Roseanne nodded.

“Okay, then. Is my car okay?”

Another nod.

The drive went by in a blur of color and sounds muted and silenced by the noise in her head—the whirlwind of legalese designed to tear her life apart.

“We’re here. Do you want me to come in with you?”

She searched the parking lot, spied his car in a VIP spot. “I don’t care.” It didn’t matter who heard what she had to say. She’d climb up on the roof and shout it to the world if it would make a difference.

She'd been here before. Nodded to the receptionist and continued down the hall to the office he'd claimed for himself when he bought the place. Behind her, she heard Kay say, "No, she'll just be a minute."

A minute. A lifetime. What did it matter? She stopped in the doorway. Scott Ramsey stood behind the desk, a cardboard box open in front of him—the desktop clear, the walls bear. Leaving. Going back to the cesspool he'd crawled out of.

He looked up, saw her. A smile on his lips that faded as his gaze swept to her swollen belly—the pregnancy unmistakable beneath the stretched out tank top she wore. "Roseanne. Sweetheart." He came toward her. "What—?"

She threw the papers at him, stopping him in his tracks. "Who the hell do you think you are? Who do you think I am? Offering me money to keep my mouth shut, to disappear into some hellhole so you can go on with your life as if nothing happened? You're despicable, Scott Ramsey. I wouldn't put your name on my child's birth certificate if someone held a gun to my head. You can tell that slimy lawyer of yours there's no charge for that, you bastard. You can keep your money. I don't want any part of it. That's the deal. The only deal you're going to get, so don't even think of suing for custody. Good luck finding me or my child if you choose that route."

Don't cry. Not now. Not yet.

"Roseanne!"

His voice spurred her on. She could barely see to walk, but she refused to cry where he might see. She'd shed enough tears over him. Never again.

"Come on. Let's get out of here."

Kay. Sweet Kay. In the car. Going. Going. Away. "Thank you."

"He's the one?"

Roseanne nodded. She closed her eyes, letting the tears fall.

~ ~ ~

Scott stood in the parking lot, legs braced apart, hands on hips, watching the car disappear with Roseanne in it. *What the fuck?* His brain scrambled to make sense of the last few seconds. He'd been packing the few things he kept in the office in order to move to his new digs in the old Cotton Exchange building. Then, as if he'd conjured her up, Roseanne stood in his doorway. Beautiful, angry, and…pregnant.

Pregnant. How the fuck had he missed that? His blood heated. He'd done that to her. Him. His baby. Their baby.

Pride, love, pure happiness coursed through his system. He'd have to call Tucker and set his ass on fire to get the house finished. They'd need a nursery. Maybe the small room next to the master suite.

"Mr. Ramsey?"

What? "What is it, Penny?"

"There's a phone call for you. It's your father. He says it's urgent."

The world stopped spinning—stilled on its axis. Everything Roseanne had said in his office came back to him in a rush that nearly brought him to his knees.

The papers. *"You can tell that slimy lawyer of yours there's no charge… You can keep your money."*

What money? He clenched his fists. His mouth felt like the Sahara as he ground his molars in an effort to keep his rage inside. His parents had somehow found out about the baby. He knew it all the way to the marrow of his bones. What had they done? "Tell him I'll call him back. Oh, and there are some papers on the floor in my office. Gather them up and bring them to me."

"Yes, sir."

The door closed behind him with a whoosh. Gaze fixed on infinity, he could see Roseanne's rounded belly as clear as day. Knew he'd do anything. Beg. Denounce his trust fund to be a father to his child.

But first, he had to find out what the hell was going on.

CHAPTER TWENTY-FOUR

"Where to?" Kay asked. They'd been driving around in circles for half an hour because Roseanne had refused to go home.

"I don't know. Home, I guess." Guests would be arriving soon, and there was no one there to greet them. Now, more than ever, she needed the inn to run smoothly. She'd need every cent she could scrape together to fight for her child. "Can you handle things by yourself this afternoon?"

"You know I can." Kay steered the car into the driveway. They walked around to the back and let themselves in through the kitchen. "I don't know about you, but I could use something cold to drink. And a cookie, maybe?" She pulled two glasses from the cabinet and filled them with sweet tea from a pitcher in the refrigerator.

Roseanne sat at the island, her hands rubbing her belly, silently telling the life within that everything would be all right. She'd find a way. Kay placed a glass in front of her then nudged the plate of cookies Roseanne had made that morning into her line of sight.

"You need to eat something. Keep your strength up."

"Thank you. For everything." Roseanne reached for a cookie. "I don't know what I would do without you."

"Good thing I'm not going anywhere, then," the older woman said.

Roseanne chuckled at the now-familiar verbal exchange. Though true, it had become their little joke. Roseanne depended on Kay, and her assistant treated her more like a daughter than an employer. They were lucky to have found each other when they had, and they both knew it.

"Things are going to get weird around

here," she said.

"What did the lawyer want?"

Over sweet tea and cookies, Roseanne filled Kay in. It was only fair the woman know what was happening since it ultimately could affect her job. If Roseanne had to disappear with her child, everything she'd built for herself would be destroyed, including the bed-and-breakfast.

"Oh, honey. That's just awful. How can people be so cruel?"

Roseanne shook her head. "I don't know, Kay. I really thought I knew Scott, but apparently I was wrong. Very, very wrong."

"Are you sure he's a part of this?"

"He was packing up his office." She met the woman's gaze. "He's going back to New York."

"Oh."

"Yeah. The bastard is running, but, just to make sure his mistake doesn't come back to bite him in the ass, he sicced his lawyer on me. Buy the lady off. Make sure his name is never mentioned in regards to his bastard child. Well, not a problem. I would…wouldn't…."

"Oh, honey." Kay embraced Roseanne. The tears she'd held at bay finally broke through the dam, spilling out in gut-wrenching sobs she had no ability to control. "It's going to be okay. Just you wait and see."

She wanted to believe that, but she was no match for the likes of the Ramseys. Money meant power, and, compared to them, she had nothing. Nothing but her determination to stay as far from them as possible.

When she finally gained some control, she could barely hold her head up. Rage, fear, and grief had stolen her strength. Kay helped her to her room and made sure she was tucked in bed. With orders to rest, Roseanne closed her eyes and slept.

She woke with a mouth as dry as cotton. The room had grown dark, but sounds coming from the floor below told her their guests for the night had arrived. Glancing at the clock, she saw she'd slept most of the day away. Her stomach rumbled, reminding her she needed to eat—not for herself but for her child. Easing her way out of bed, she stretched and gingerly made her way to her private bathroom. After a quick shower, she pulled her hair back and dressed in leggings and a flowing top that didn't scream pregnant woman.

Taking the back stairs to the kitchen, she hoped to avoid seeing anyone. She should have known Kay would be there.

"There you are. I made dinner for you. It's not much, just soup and some of that bread you made the other day. I used that recipe you were working on last month. I hope you aren't sick of Minestrone."

"No. I'm not sick of it." She'd adapted the iconic Italian soup, adding meat and thickening the sauce to make a hearty main dish version. "Thanks."

"Not a problem. Have a seat. It'll just take a few minutes to heat it up." She turned a burner on beneath a giant stockpot then set about getting a bowl and utensils.

Roseanne helped herself to a glass of water, drinking it down in one long gulp before refilling it and sitting down to wait for her meal. If she got to keep the advance the publishing company had paid her, she would have to consider using a portion of it to make things easier for her assistant. Kay had spent too many nights sleeping on the loveseat in Roseanne's office. Maybe she would consider moving into the owner's suite on the third floor once the garage had been converted to an apartment for her and the baby.

The child seemed to do a somersault, startling her and bringing back into focus the painful reality she now had to live with. Scott didn't want anything to do with his child.

A buzzing sound drew her attention to the corner of the island. A cell phone vibrated on the polished marble surface.

"It's been ringing all afternoon. I put it on silent so it wouldn't disturb the guests."

"Who?"

Kay shrugged and continued to stir the soup. "Don't know. None of my business."

Roseanne retrieved the phone, waiting until she was seated to punch the button that would bring the screen to life. *Scott.* Twenty-seven times. He'd left a couple of voicemails and a few dozen text messages, too. She set the phone aside. Whatever he had to say could wait until she had eaten. Maybe even forever. "Everything go okay with check-in?"

"Yep. Couple in the front room were late getting in, but everyone is settled now. The couple in the Senator's Suite want to talk to you about having their daughter's wedding here in the spring. Said they saw pictures of the Adams's wedding in some magazine and thought this would be the perfect place."

"I'll talk to them tomorrow. Anything else?"

"Nope. You going to be alright this evening? I can stay if you think you need me."

"I'm good." If Scott decided to come over instead of harass her by phone, she'd call the police. She didn't have to take any shit from him or his family. "Thanks for everything. I don't know what

I'd do without you."

The older woman slid a bowl of soup and a generous slice of homemade bread in front of her. "Good thing I'm not going anywhere, then."

~ ~ ~

How the hell did his life get this fucked up?

Scott read the offer again. And again, his blood pressure hit the roof. He'd tried countless times to contact Roseanne, let her know this was bullshit and to forget about it, but she hadn't answered a single one of his calls or texted him back. He had no idea if she'd listened to the voicemail messages he'd left. He could only hope she had.

He'd wanted to go to her, tell her in person, but as soon as he'd read the papers she'd thrown at him, he'd known the only way to end this was in person. As the wheels of his private jet skidded on the runway, he gripped the armrests and steeled himself for the confrontation to come. If the people who shared his blood couldn't accept him, the woman he loved, and the child they'd created, then they could go to hell. And they could take their money with them. He had enough of his own. More than they knew. Maybe more than all of them combined.

While he'd worked hard and made wise investments that had netted him a sizeable fortune, they'd spent. Lavish parties. Expensive toys, vacations, and clothes. None of that meant anything to him. He'd rather barbeque in the backyard with a few friends than put on a tux and mingle with a bunch of people who thought they were better than anyone else. He'd gladly give up his jet for a car and a long trip with Roseanne along the back roads of Texas. Give him a pair of jeans and an old T-shirt, and he would be a happy man.

Pretenses were for those who had no identity of their own. He knew exactly who he was, and, in a few minutes, his family would know, too.

He rented a car at the airport. He'd called no one. He was here for one reason, and when he'd completed his task, he would leave. Maybe forever. That was up to them. He no longer cared what decision they made as long as they left him the hell alone. Because, as soon as he cleared this matter up, he was going home. To Texas. To Roseanne. To his child. To the future he had always wanted.

He didn't ring the bell. Didn't wait for Curtis to let him in. Who the hell needed a butler? Open your own damned door. How difficult was that?

"Mom! Dad!"

Curtis, his brows raised in alarm, appeared at the end of the long, center hallway. "Mr. Ramsey! We weren't expecting you."

No shit. "Where are they?"

"I believe Mrs. Ramsey is upstairs. Mr. Ramsey is out at the putting green. The weather—"

"Tell them both I'll be waiting in the library. If they aren't there in five minutes, they'll be hearing from my attorney tomorrow."

Curtis dipped his chin. "As you wish." Then he was gone, leaving Scott standing in the middle of the marble monstrosity his parents called a home.

He shook his head. He couldn't wait to move into the old Victorian he'd purchased. Tucker had assured him the renovation would be complete in two weeks. He'd laughed and asked for a realistic estimate. "Okay, four weeks," the man had said. "Promise."

His sneakers squeaked on the polished floor as he made his way to the library. Lined with books and furnished with warm leather chairs, it was the only room in the house he truly liked. Though smaller, the library in his new house would look much the same as this one, and double as a home office he would share with Roseanne—if he could convince her to marry him. After the stunt his parents had pulled, he couldn't predict what would happen when he asked her. Once, he'd had no doubt.

He'd screwed that up all on his own. His intentions had been good. Spot-on as this latest debacle proved. He'd been right to protect Roseanne from his family. If she'd let him, he'd protect her for the rest of their lives.

At the sound of footsteps on the

marble floor outside, Scott turned. His parents entered through the double doors together. If he'd had any doubt they were in this together, their united front banished it.

"Scott, darling," his mother said. "We're so glad you're home."

"Son," his father said. "You should have called. We would have sent Robert to pick you up."

"I'm perfectly capable of driving myself. As a matter of fact, I'm capable of doing a lot of things. Like choosing where I will live. What I will do with my time and my money. I can even dress myself and cook my own food." He nodded. "Shocking, I know. I even do my own laundry."

"Scott—"

He held up a hand to stop his mother. "You know what else I can do? I can choose who I want to be my family."

"Now, son—"

"Don't. Don't call me that. You've lost the right." Scott clenched his fists to keep from picking up something and throwing it across the room. Venting his anger like a spoiled child would only convince these two they'd done the right thing. "How dare you make decisions for me concerning the people I love? How dare you assume I have no right to raise my own child? What did you think you would do with the baby if Roseanne refused to take your money? Huh? Did you think you'd sue for custody then ship the kid off to boarding schools for the rest of its life? Pretend it didn't exist?"

He could see from the look on their faces he'd hit that nail on the head. His stomach turned. "Let me tell you how this is going to go. You are going to call your lawyer and tell him this was all a big mistake. You're going to tell him to destroy everything to do with this ridiculous proceeding. He's to forget he ever laid eyes on Roseanne Meadows. Then you're going to forget you ever met her, and while you're at it, you're going to forget about me. I don't exist as far as you're concerned. Don't try to contact me. Ever. Is that clear?"

"Perfectly, brother of mine."

Scott's gaze shot to his sister who

stood in the doorway. He had no proof she had anything to do with this, but he had his suspicions. Trouble might as well have been her middle name. "Ronnie."

"So you knocked up the little innkeeper." She shrugged and stepped into the room. "No big deal. Happens all the time." She moved like a cat on the prowl. He tracked her movements, determined not to become her prey again.

"You will speak with respect where Roseanne is concerned, or you won't speak at all. And it is a big deal to me. That's my child you're talking about, not to mention the woman I love."

"Love? Really, Scotty? She's a mouse. Don't you think you've toyed with her enough? It's time to cut your losses before you find yourself living in that mouse hole of a town, playing daddy to a litter of squeaky kids."

He dug his nails into the palms of his hands. He'd never struck a person in anger before, but if she didn't stop talking, she might just be the first. Woman or not. "Shut up while you still can, Ronnie."

"Mom and Dad did you a favor. Why can't you see that? You know, Solange has been asking about you? She's yours for the asking. Think about it. She'd be the perfect wife for you. She's beautiful. She has her own life. She wouldn't drag you down."

He'd dated the supermodel for several months and couldn't recall a single moment of their time together. All he remembered was feeling like a noose had been looped around his neck, the end of the rope held tight by his mother and his grandmother's goddamned china. "You want me to marry her so the two of you can continue fucking each other without anyone knowing."

"What?" his mother screeched.

"Here now!" his father bellowed.

"Fuck you." This came from his sister.

Bingo. He'd nailed that one, too. "Don't worry. I'm not going to tell anyone as long as you and them"—he indicated his parents who were now staring at their youngest child—"leave me and my *family* alone."

"We're your family, dickwad."

"No. You aren't. Family doesn't try to make their grandchildren disappear. They don't manipulate their children's or sibling's lives. I'm done with all of you. As Davy Crockett said, 'You may all go to hell, and I will go to Texas.'"

He shoved his way past his speechless parents and fuming sister. Veronica chased him to the front door, alternately swearing at him and begging him not to say anything about her relationship with Solange. He had nothing left to say, so he kept his mouth shut. Halfway back to the airport, he pulled into a service center and peeled his fingers from the steering wheel. He went in and grabbed a cup of coffee and a donut. The coffee tasted like dirty water and the pastry might have been cardboard. He didn't care. The caffeine and sugar gave him the energy to continue on toward the new life he'd chosen for himself.

Returning to the freeway, he thought about what he'd just done. He wasn't happy about cutting ties with his family, but it was the only way he could see to go forward. He wouldn't poison his new life with the negative energy he'd lived with his entire life. He wanted more for Roseanne and his son or daughter. But first, he had to convince Roseanne to talk to him. Or at least hear him out. Until he could accomplish that, his life would be on hold.

CHAPTER TWENTY-FIVE

"Becky?" Scott stood in Becky Jean Parker-Adams's office doorway, his fists clenched almost as tight as his jaw. He'd had exactly twenty-four hours to think about the fact he was going to be a father, and that others had known and kept it from him. One of those people sat before him. "Have you got a minute?"

She smiled and shoved her computer keyboard tray under the desk. "Sure. I could use a break."

Scott stepped inside, shutting the door behind him. Becky raised an eyebrow, but kept her smile in place. He understood her first loyalty would be to Roseanne, and, though he was certain

Becky had known about the baby for some time, it was her love for her best friend that he was counting on today.

"Mind if I sit?"

"Not at all. What's on your mind? Is this about the new offices? Ford told me you'd shown him some space downtown."

He sat in one of the ancient chairs in front of her equally ancient desk. "No, this isn't about the office space, though you really should consider relocating your corporate offices. Having everything under one roof would make life a lot easier for you."

"I agree. That's why we're going ahead with the purchase of the property you brought to our attention. We had your man, Mr. Tucker, walk through it with us. It's not going to be cheap, but renovations are possible."

Scott nodded. "I'm glad to hear that." He met her gaze head-on. "Is there some other news you would like to tell me? Maybe something I should know but is being kept from me?"

She held his gaze for a moment

before she closed her eyes and sighed. "I told her she should have told you. How did you find out?"

So, she did know. "She came to my office yesterday, basically to tell me I could go to hell."

Becky sat forward, her eyebrows knit together. "Why would she do that?"

"Because my parents' lawyer paid her a visit. Presented her with an offer—money enough to live on for a few years in exchange for filling in unknown under father's name on the birth certificate and never acknowledging to anyone that I'm the father. The papers she threw at me said if she didn't accept the offer, they'd sue for custody and she'd never see her child again."

Becky's mouth hung open. Her eyes had grown wide and her face pale. "You can't be serious."

"I had nothing to do with it. I didn't know she was pregnant, and I haven't got a clue how my parents found out. The only time they met her was at your wedding, and it certainly wasn't obvious then."

"No, it wasn't. She's only recently begun to show." Becky slumped in her chair.

"How far along is she?"

"Five months."

He did the calculation in his head. "Before Vegas."

Becky nodded. "Yes. She found out shortly after the Vegas trip."

"She was sick. Morning sickness?"

"Yeah. She didn't know at first. I actually figured it out and had to convince her to take a test."

He'd missed experiencing that with her, and so much more. "She's been to a doctor?"

Becky opened her mouth to speak then shut it. She studied him for a moment then tried again. "You really should be talking to her about this. It's not my place—"

"No, it's not your place. However, Roseanne made it clear yesterday she doesn't want to see me. I swear to you, I didn't know. None of the things my parents threatened in those papers will ever happen. I won't let them happen. I intend to be a father to my child, but, first, I have to talk to Roseanne. I need your help to do that."

She picked up a pen and twirled it between her fingers. "Ford said you're planning to stay in Butte Plains."

"I am. This is my home now, even if things don't work out between me and Roseanne, but I can tell you, I want them to."

"Okay." She nodded. "I believe you. I always thought the two of you were good together, but she's my best friend. Just because you're Ford's best friend doesn't mean I'll cut you any slack. You've hurt her before. If you do it again, I'll make it my job to make your life here a living hell. Understood?"

"Understood. Now, will you talk to her? Convince her to hear me out?"

"I'll do my best, but there might be an issue."

"What kind of issue?"

"I thought I was the only person besides Roseanne to know. She hasn't even told her parents."

"Or me."

"Or you. She might think I told someone…maybe Ford, and that he told you. It would be a logical assumption."

Scott rolled his shoulders to ease the growing tension there. "I see what you mean."

"I hope she knows I would never do anything like that, but hormones seem to rule her these days. I'll do my best, if she'll talk to me."

That was the most he could hope for. "Thank you. You'll let me know how it works out?"

"I'll call you after I've talked to her—if I talk to her." Scott rose. He'd made it to the door when she stopped him. "Oh, and, Scott?"

"Yeah?"

"You'd better figure out how your family got wind of this. Roseanne isn't going to take kindly to having these people looking over her shoulder."

~ ~ ~

Damn. She shouldn't have left those papers in Scott's office. Not that she'd ever forget what they said, but her lawyer would want to read them for himself. She ran a finger over the raised lettering on the business card the Ramsey's shyster had left behind. Her attorney could call and get all the details he needed. If she never saw or heard from a Ramsey again, it would be too soon.

She didn't know where she was going to get the kind of money she'd need to fight the Ramsey's, but she would. Absolutely no one was going to take her child away. She'd work ten jobs if she needed.

She had to make some decisions about the running of the bed-and-breakfast. The more she thought about it, the more it made sense to convert the garage into an apartment for herself and the baby, or a future caretaker. That would open up all the bedrooms in the house to guests, increasing potential income. The first step would be to get an expert's opinion on the garage conversion. She dug through the top drawer of her desk and found Randy Tucker's business card. If anyone would know if her idea would work, it would be him. She'd been flattered by the personal interest he'd shown in her, but one look at her now would squash that. Too bad. In another life, she probably would have gone out with him.

Before she could talk herself out of it, she dialed the number on the card. Expecting it to go to voicemail, she jumped when the line connected, his voice sounding distant. "I'll be right back. Don't do anything until I tell you to." A moment later, he spoke into the phone. "Randy Tucker. How can I help you?"

"Mr. Tucker. It's Roseanne Meadows. From The Yellow Rose Bed-and-Breakfast?"

"Oh, hello. How are you?"

"I'm fine. You?"

"I wish just once a client wouldn't change their mind in the middle of a renovation, but, other than that, everything is good."

"Oh. I'm sorry. I mean, I thought I'd get your voicemail. I can call back later."

"No problem. I needed to get something out of my truck anyway. What's up?"

"I was wondering if you could come by

sometime—no real hurry—and give me some advice. I'm thinking about converting my detached garage into an apartment. I don't know where to begin or if it's even something that could be done."

"You'd have to check with the city to make sure it's allowed. No use spending money on architectural drawings if the city won't approve the construction."

"I hadn't thought of that." A car door opened in the background. After a short interval, it slammed shut.

"I'm just around the corner from you. I could drop by in about an hour and take a look. No sense going to all the trouble of checking with the city if the building isn't structurally sound to begin with."

She could feel a headache coming on. None of the things he'd mentioned had even occurred to her. "Would you mind? I'd really appreciate it. I don't want to waste a lot of time and money on a dead end."

"Let me make sure my crew is clear on the changes the owner wants to make then I'll be over. Expect me within the hour, okay?"

"Perfect. Thanks, Mr. Tucker."

"Randy. You can call me Randy."

"Thanks, Randy."

"See you soon, Roseanne." The line went dead.

The interest he'd clearly shown in her when they first met hadn't gone away. She caressed her belly. *It will soon enough. Just wait until he gets a good look at me now.*

When he called to say he was on his way, Roseanne met him in front of the garage. Painted yellow with white trim to match the house, the two-car structure hadn't been touched in decades other than to add a fresh coat of paint when needed. The matching barn-style doors had long since succumbed to gravity, hanging slightly off-kilter.

"Sorry to keep you waiting," Randy said, stepping through the break in the hedges that led to the alley.

"Not a problem. Seriously. This could wait."

His gaze took her in, stopping briefly on the mound beneath her shirt she could no longer hide. "I don't know. Looks like you'll be needing an extra room pretty soon."

Heat rushed to her cheeks. She hadn't gotten used to people's reactions yet, especially from those who knew she wasn't married. Placing a protective hand on her belly, she summoned her inner strength. "Yes, I was thinking I could turn this into an apartment for myself. That would free up the room I'm currently using for another guest room. I just don't know if it's feasible or if I can afford to do it. It's worth checking into, I guess."

"What kind of timeline are you thinking?"

Roseanne shrugged. "I don't know. I guess it depends on how much it would cost. I'd have to see about getting financing to cover it then there's the city. I have no idea if they'll let me convert the garage or not."

"Well, let's take a look. There are a few key things to watch out for when you're thinking of doing something like this." He walked to the corner of the building. "I'd say you have about five hundred square feet, give or take." His gaze went to the roofline. "Not enough clearance there to make a second story, but you might get another two hundred square feet of loft space. My best guess is it would be a total of around six hundred square feet finished. Not huge, but enough for the essentials."

"I could put in a kitchen and a bathroom, right?"

"There's electricity," he said, pointing to the overhead wire running from the pole in the alley. "What about water and sewer?"

She shook her head. "Not that I know of."

"That would be something to figure into the cost. Let's have a look inside."

Roseanne kept the door hinges oiled, so the big door swung easily, as long as she lifted the end up so it didn't drag in the dirt. They stepped inside. Randy paid no attention to the boxes stacked around the perimeter. Some of them still contained things Roseanne had brought with her when she'd moved back from Florida years ago. Others were things her grandparents had collected over the years. She'd always said she would go through them, but hadn't found the time yet. If she were to go ahead with the construction, she'd have to find time. Everything in here would have to be moved. That meant she'd need a new storage place for the gardening tools and lawn mower, too.

"The roof looks sound, inside and out, but I'd have to get up on it to really tell."

"It's at least fifteen years old. I think my grandmother had it replaced at the same time she had the one on the house redone."

Randy nodded. "It should be okay, then. That would save you a lot of money." He poked around at the exposed studs. No one had ever bothered to finish the walls. "The wood looks to be in good condition. No rot that I can see. No evidence of termite damage. You'd need to reinforce the joists if you were to put a loft in. Electrical isn't up to today's code. That would all have to be redone. Depending on the floor plan you choose, you might have to put in more windows. Every bedroom has to have an accessible window in case of fire. You'd have to seal up the front, get rid of those garage doors and put in a regular door."

"That sounds like a lot of work and expense."

"On a place this size, it wouldn't take all that long. Three weeks, maybe four. If you want, I can draw up a rough estimate. Something you could take to the bank for the loan."

Looking at the project through his eyes made it seem impossible. Why had she ever thought this could be a solution to her problem? "Let me think about it. I guess I should check and see if the city will let me do it first. An estimate at this point would be putting the cart before the horse."

"I know it sounds like a lot, but it would be a piece of cake for an experienced contractor. See what the city has to say, and if they're okay with it, let me know. I think I know this guy who owns a construction company, and he just happens to have a crew in the neighborhood. I bet I could talk him into giving you a good price."

She could feel heat blooming on her cheeks. "Thank you. I wouldn't expect any favors. That's not why I called you."

"I know, but you've been a big help to me on this project. Thanks to you, your neighbor is going to have an authentically restored home. I owe you."

"You don't owe me anything. How's the house coming? Almost finished?"

"We're getting there. We'd be done upstairs if the owner hadn't thrown a curveball yesterday."

"Oh?"

"Yeah. Said he wanted to add a door between the master bedroom and the guest room next to it."

"Why would they want to do something like that?"

"Word is they just found out they're going to have a baby. They want to use the guest room as a nursery and thought a connecting door would be convenient."

It had to be a coincidence. That was all it was. "Did you ever find out who the owner is?"

"Nope. All my communication is through Riley. Hey, did you ever contact him?"

She shook her head. "No. Once I saw what you were doing with the house, I forgot. You said the company owns more property in town?"

"Yeah. A whole city block downtown and some other stuff we aren't involved with. We just finished the building they're going to use for their offices. That Cotton Exchange must have been something back in the day. It's pretty special now."

"I remember you saying you were going to do that restoration, too. I'd love to see it."

"You should stop by sometime. Riley said they'd be all moved in by the end of this week. I'm sure he'd love to show you around."

"Thanks. I might do that. I need to go downtown anyway to talk to someone about the zoning issue."

He glanced at the screen on his phone. "Sorry, but I've got to run. I need to locate a vintage pocket door so my crew can get it installed. All of a sudden, the owner wants this place done yesterday."

"Must be the new baby. I know I'm sure thinking about the future."

"Anything you need, Roseanne. Just let me know."

She fought back tears as she watched him disappear through the break in the hedges. She'd detected nothing but genuine kindness in his words and manner. Her heart hurt with the realization a virtual stranger had more compassion for her circumstances than the father of her child. Why hadn't she met him first? He was the kind of guy she should have fallen in love with, but love wasn't something one controlled. Just the opposite. It made otherwise sane people do insane things.

No need living in the past. What's done is done. Time to look to the future. She replaced the lock on the garage doors and headed back to the house to contemplate her next move. Should she go downtown and ask about the zoning? That was the first hurdle. If she couldn't get a permit to convert the garage, she'd have to come up with another solution to her problem.

"Then that's where I'll start," she mumbled to herself. She'd just reached the back porch when her phone rang. She recognized the ringtone assigned to her best friend and hesitated. She'd tried not to think about how Scott had found out about the baby, but unless he'd seen her recently, which to her knowledge he hadn't, then someone had to have told him. Since the only other person in town who knew was Becky, it stood to reason her oldest friend had let the secret slip. Maybe to her husband who was Scott's best friend. She'd said from the beginning Roseanne should tell Scott. Well, now he knew, and look how that had turned out.

Roseanne hit the ignore button and slipped the phone into her pocket. She needed a little more time before she forgave Becky.

CHAPTER TWENTY-SIX

It had been weeks since she'd been downtown. Construction trucks bearing the logo of Tucker Restoration lined one side of Main between Second and Third. Though the windows of the old corner store were covered in heavy paper, the door stood open. Roseanne peeked inside. An army of people were busy restoring the ancient wood trim while still others worked on what appeared to be a bar against the far wall.

She'd missed more Historical Society meetings than she'd been able to attend in the last six months. From the looks of it, she'd missed quite a lot. All along the block, windows sparkled in the sunlight, sidewalks had been repaired, light poles bore a fresh coat of paint, and baskets filled with vibrant flowers hung from new brackets. If not for the modern vehicles parked along the road, she would have thought she'd stepped back in time to the turn of the twentieth century when cotton had ruled this part of Texas.

Moving along, she came to a stop in front of the old Cotton Exchange building. The window still held the original glass, imperfections and all, but, now, the ornate gold lettering declared the building to be the home of BP Investments, Inc.

She pressed her face close to the glass, but not close enough to leave a smudge, and peered inside. The front part appeared to be some sort of waiting area. Large, masculine leather chairs were arranged into seating areas around tables that looked like slices from giant tree trunks. Plush rugs covered wide-plank hardwood floors and defined the arrangements. "Wow." Someone had spent a truckload of money to make the place appear casual yet elegant.

A tall, slim man walked into the room.

He carried an electronic tablet in one hand, which he consulted as he negotiated the furniture. Roseanne jumped back. The man glanced up, saw her standing outside, and smiled at her. He set the tablet on a large, wooden desk at the back of the room then headed toward her, motioning for her to enter.

She shook her head. She really shouldn't. City Hall would be closing down for lunch soon, and she wanted to make her inquiries and get home before today's guests began arriving. Not that Kay needed her to be there, but it was her inn, and she felt responsible for everything that went on there. Before she could convince her feet to move, the man opened the front door—original front door, she noted.

"Want to take a closer look? It's okay. I think just about everyone in town has been in the last few days to see the place. We're still moving in, but I'd be happy to show you around."

"Really? It wouldn't be too much trouble?" Why was she even asking? She was dying to see what they'd done with the place. "I'm a member of the Historical Society."

"Then you have to come in. It's the law or something, isn't it?"

His smile and good humor lifted her spirits. What would it hurt to spend a few minutes checking out the restoration? "Okay. If you're sure? I don't want to get in your way."

"I'm positive. Have you lived here long?" he asked as she walked past him into the room.

"All my life. Well, most of it anyway. We moved to Florida when I was in high school, but I came back as soon as I could."

"Then you probably know some of the history of the building and the others on the block."

She nodded. "I do. This was a five-and-dime when I was a kid. I guess the dollar stores are the modern day equivalent." She ran her hand over the rich wood panels that still graced the walls. She pointed to the ornate marble stairway off to one side. "I used to love that staircase. It looked like something out of a fairy tale, or so I thought when I was ten. I'm glad to see it survived."

"I was given permission to murder anyone who dared mar that staircase, or any other original pieces. I'm happy to say I didn't have to kill anyone. Tucker Restoration did a wonderful job of bringing the place into this century without destroying the history of the building."

Roseanne laughed. "The owner must really like his historical details."

"He does."

The familiar voice froze her in her tracks. Her heart did a somersault just as the baby decided to shift positions. She gasped and, arm outstretched, braced herself against the wall.

"Roseanne!" Scott flew to her side. "Are you okay?" He took her elbow and guided her to the nearest chair—a big, tan leather job that looked like it could seat a football team. "Riley. Get Ms. Meadows a glass of water."

"Yes, sir." The other gentleman scooted off to do as Scott commanded.

"I'm fine. I don't need water." She tried

to wrench out of his embrace, but, with one arm around her waist and the other firmly holding her elbow, she didn't have a chance. She sat where he indicated, hoping he'd move away, giving her a chance to escape. No such luck. He sat on the edge of the cushion, effectively trapping her in the chair.

"You're pale."

"I'm fine. I just didn't expect to see you here."

"I thought— Becky didn't talk to you?"

She shook her head. "No. Why?" She remembered the earlier call she'd sent to voicemail. She'd never even checked to see if she'd left a message. "Is she okay?"

"She's fine, or at least she was when I saw her this morning."

"Then why would you think she and I would have talked?"

Riley came back with a cut crystal glass filled with water and ice. Scott took it then handed it to her. "Why don't you go see how things are going down the street?" he said with a nod toward the door. "I'm sure I can handle anything that comes up in the next few minutes."

"Sure thing, boss. Oh, and Randy called. Something about a pocket door. He said you should call him."

"I'll take care of it."

Riley swung his hips as he made his way to the door. "Okeydokey, then. I think I'll take my lunch break while I'm out. Don't wait up for me."

Scott waved to his employee, and when the man was out of sight, he turned to Roseanne, a big smile on his face that vanished quickly. "What's the matter? Is it the baby? Are you having contractions?"

"Fuck you, Scott Ramsey. How dare you act like you care a fig about my baby."

His expression turned thunderous. "That's *our* baby, and I care a hell of a lot more than a fig, whatever that means."

"I didn't come here to argue with you." She made an attempt to get out of the chair, but between the deep cushions and Scott's big body wedged in beside her, she couldn't leverage herself out. "Move!"

"You aren't going anywhere until we talk."

"I'll call the police. This is kidnapping."

"It's nothing even close. You came into my place of business of your own free will."

"And you won't let me leave. That's kidnapping."

"If Becky didn't talk to you, why are you here?"

"Randy said the building was finished. I just came to see it. I didn't know—" She cut herself off as something Riley had said finally penetrated her brain. "You! The pocket door. You're the one who bought the Victorian around the corner from me."

"Guilty as charged."

He'd told Randy to add a pocket door between the master bedroom and the guest room next to it because he wanted to make the smaller room into a nursery. "If you think you're going to take my child away from me and raise it on the next street over, you really are insane. I'll fight you until my last breath then I'll come back from the dead to haunt you." She made another attempt to get up. "Get out of my way!"

"Hold on, Roseanne. You aren't going anywhere until you get it through your thick skull that I'm not your enemy. I bought that house months ago, along with a lot of other properties, to prove to you that I'm not going anywhere. I have a Texas driver's license, which Ford assures me makes me almost a Texan. I own property here. When you saw me at the factory yesterday, I was packing things to move in here."

"I thought—"

"You thought I was going back to New York. I know. You didn't give me a chance to explain."

Could she have been wrong about him? "Why do you want a nursery?"

"I thought it would make it easier on you to have direct access to the baby's room. Is that a crime?"

She shook her head. "You expect me to live there? I have a home, Scott."

"You have a business. It's not a suitable place to raise a kid, not with strangers coming and going all the time.

I bought the house for us, before I knew about the baby, but it's yours, with or without me."

"Scott—"

"No argument. The house is in your name, anyway."

"Why did you do that?"

"I thought it would make a nice wedding gift."

"You were going to ask me to marry you?"

He nodded. "In Vegas. Then you got sick and asked to come home."

She recalled the reason she'd felt sick that night—or at least the reason she'd thought she felt sick. "You didn't tell me about the party."

"My parents' anniversary?"

She nodded.

"I didn't want to subject you to their brand of hospitality. You've met them, and after that visit from their lawyer, surely you can understand why I didn't want you anywhere near them."

His parents had been civil when they'd been in town for Ford and Becky's wedding, but just barely. They hadn't even left a tip for the housekeeper when they checked out, despite being a pain in the ass, complaining about everything from the size of the bath towels to the creaking floors. "I guess I can, but still, you should have told me. Let me make up my own mind."

His brows met in the center of his forehead. "For the record, how did you know about it in the first place?"

"Your sister made a point of telling me in Vegas. I'm sorry, but she's a piece of work."

"I know. Can you believe Ford dated her?"

"No. She's a viper."

"Takes after my parents."

"Can I ask you something?"

"Shoot."

"How did you find out about the baby? Did Becky tell you?"

"You told me."

She recalled the stunned expression on his face. "No way. You mean you didn't know until yesterday?"

"Didn't have a clue, which makes me wonder how my parents found out."

"Well, I sure as hell didn't tell them." They both thought about the problem for minute. "Wait. I was in New York last week. You think they could have seen me and I didn't see them?"

"It's a big city. Lots of people. Why were you there, and where did you go?"

"I went to meet with my agent and my publisher. I sold the cookbook I've been working on." She grabbed his arm and squeezed. "You didn't have anything to do with that, did you?"

"I might have called an old friend, made a suggestion. What's your agent's name?"

"Liz Rothstein with the Greenberg Agency."

"Never heard of her or her agency."

"Are you sure?"

"Positive. Even if my friend did put a bug in someone's ear there, I can tell you those people don't sign contracts as favors to anyone. They think your book will sell, or they wouldn't buy it."

"Uh-huh. I don't believe you, but I've got other things to worry about."

"Like finding out how my parents knew

about the baby before I did. You can't imagine how pissed off that makes me."

"I would have told you—"

"But my sister came along, stirring up trouble. It's what she does best."

"I didn't know in Vegas. I honestly was sick. Turns out it was morning sickness."

"And you weren't showing at Ford and Becky's wedding. I would have noticed."

She didn't need a mirror to know her ears and neck were turning red. He couldn't have gotten a better look that night. "It didn't even occur to me that you might notice."

"All I remember is how beautiful you were. You were a vision in pink, and when I touched you… Well, I had to have you."

"When you touch me—"

"What?" His fingers skimmed her arm from wrist to elbow. "What happens when I touch you?"

"You know." His hand moved slowly along, barely touching her skin.

"I don't." He leaned in. His lips brushed the shell of her ear. "Tell me, sweetheart."

"I…can't." If he got any closer, she might combust. That was what he did to her.

Hot breath stirred the hair tucked behind her ear. "It makes you hot, doesn't it?" He took her earlobe between his lips and sucked gently on the sensitive skin. "At the wedding…you were hot for me. Wet." He nibbled down her neck to her collar then back up. "When I put the garter on your leg, I could smell your arousal. You wanted me then, didn't you?"

Her actions had proved that point, so there was no need to deny it now. "Yes."

His tongue traced her carotid, making her pulse jump like a racehorse out of the chute. "I still have the panties I took off of you that night."

God, she had felt like such a slut going back to the wedding without them. Every brush of air against her swollen, slicked skin had reminded her of the mistake she'd made. Mistake.

She gathered all her strength and pushed against his chest. He sat back, his face a mask of confusion. Well, she'd clear that up for him. "Yet, two days later you were out with another woman. Did you have my panties with you then? Were you thinking about me then?" She heaved herself past him and stood. "I don't think so."

CHAPTER TWENTY-SEVEN

"Roseanne." He stood, his hands outstretched, pleading with her. "Honestly, I don't know what you're talking about. What woman? Where?"

"Don't." She held her hands up, palms out. "Don't deny it. I was there. At the diner. I saw you, Scott. Me. With my own eyes."

She knew the second comprehension dawned on him. His facial muscles sagged, and his gaze dropped to the floor. "Yeah. Did you think no one you knew would see you out there by the freeway? Is that why you took her there?"

"It's not what you think."

"I think you're screwing Julie Davis.

That's what I think."

He planted his fists on his hips and glared at her. "That was a business meeting. Julie came downtown earlier to look over the corner space as a possible location for a tasting room. The diner was her idea because she had to go into Dallas for supplies after our appointment. We had our heads together over a sketch pad. Would you like to see the original drawings she did that day? Or the architect's final drawings that came from that meeting? How about we go over there and I'll show you how the construction is coming along? Oh." He reached in the front pocket of his jeans. "Yes, I had your panties with me that day. I carry them with me every day."

She stared at the ball of white lace and satin sitting in the palm of his hand. She didn't know what to say. He had an answer for everything she threw at him, and they all sounded plausible. Had she been wrong about him? About everything? "Why?"

"Why do I carry them?"

She nodded.

"To remind me of what's at stake here. To remind me of my goal."

Her gaze me his. "You're goal?"

"To get you back. I'm nothing without you, Roseanne. You never believed I'd stick, but you were wrong. This is my home, and not because I own property or have a Texas driver's license, but because this is where you are. I bought the leather factory, this building, the airstrip, for you. You love this town, every crumbling brick of it. I'd restore the whole damned place for you if I could."

"You would?"

He stuffed her panties back in his pocket. "I'd do anything for you, Roseanne. Anything. You want me to beg you to take me back? I'll do it. I rented about a dozen billboards along the freeway. I'll have them plastered with signs begging you. I'd run naked down Main Street just to see your eyes light up. I love you."

"You do?"

"More than is wise. I told my family to fuck off because of you. That lawyer who came to see you is probably trying to figure out a way to cut me out of my inheritance as we speak."

"Oh, Scott. No!"

"I don't care, Roseanne. My parents have never understood me. My grandparents did. They were good people, kept my parents in line. But once they were gone…well, things changed. My parents' expectations for me are so far out of line with what I want for myself, I can't see them ever coming together."

"But, the money."

"Means nothing to me. I have plenty of my own, and they can't touch my trust funds. At the rate they're spending their own money, there won't be anything left to inherit when they're gone anyway." He shook his head. "I don't get it. If they were spending it on a good cause—"

"Like bringing a dead town back to life?"

He smiled. "Yeah, like bringing a dead town back to life, I wouldn't have a problem with their spending. But all they can think about is themselves. I'd much rather invest in Butte Plains. Did you see how great Main Street looks? That was community volunteers. I bought the supplies, but the people in town did the heavy lifting. I respect their work ethic, Roseanne. The town has been through hard times, but the people who live here, like you, haven't given up. They're bringing it back to life themselves. They just needed a little help."

"You're enjoying this, aren't you?"

His smile lit up the room. "I am. Do you remember when you told me about this building? How you used to come here when you were a kid?"

"I remember."

"I decided to buy the building then. I have to admit, I wasn't planning on buying an entire city block, but, once I started looking into it, it made sense."

"So, Lucky Lady Brewing will have a tasting room on the corner. Your offices are here? What are you going to do with the space in between?"

"Want to see what I have in mind?"

"Sure."

"Let me get the keys, and the plans I had drawn up." He started to head upstairs but stopped on the first tread.

"Want to see what we did upstairs?"

Why not? She'd always dreamed of what this building could be in the right hands. "Okay." Following him up the ornate staircase, she marveled at the condition of the woodwork. "Is this all original?"

"It is. Took forever to get all the layers of paint off, but it was worth it, don't you think?"

"Yes. It's beautiful. All this was made by hand."

"Over a hundred and fifty years ago. It's a testament to the craftsmanship and quality of wood they used that it's still here."

"And you. If you hadn't bought the place, no telling what would have happened to it."

"You gave me the idea, so all this is your fault."

They reached the switchback landing. Scott stopped and waited for her to catch up. She placed her fingers on his arm. "Seriously, Scott. You aren't spending your entire fortune on my dream, are you?"

His gaze bored into hers. "I would, if it would bring you back to me, but no. I haven't even made a dent in it. Besides, I expect to make it all back, except for what I'm spending on the house. That's for you and the baby."

And maybe for him, too, but she wasn't ready to go there just yet. "Thank you." She stepped past him and continued to the second story.

"What do you think?" He came up behind her. "The infrastructure is all new, wiring, plumbing, but, otherwise, it's exactly the way we found it."

"It's...beautiful." Low, natural wood walls separated the front room into individual work spaces occupied by vintage desks topped by ultra-modern computer systems. Most had ergonomic chairs behind the desks, but a few still had old-fashioned wooden ones. An office sectioned off with the same low, wood walls topped with frosted glass took up the entire back wall. "Your office?"

"My office. Want to see?"

It was modern and historically perfect in every way possible. Roseanne circled the massive carved oak desk, taking in every detail, including a photo of her that had been taken at Becky and Ford's first wedding in Las Vegas. The photographer had caught her in an unguarded moment when she'd smiled at something one of them had said.

"You were so beautiful." He'd followed her around the desk. He picked up the frame and gazed at the photo. "I didn't think it was possible for you to be any more beautiful, but I was wrong. Pregnancy suits you. You're radiant."

"I'm a blimp."

"No. You don't know what it does to me to see you like this. My child growing inside you. A child conceived of our love. No matter what happens between you and me, I'll always love and care for you and the baby. I'll always be right here, Roseanne."

She ducked her head to keep him from seeing the tears gathering in her eyes. "Thank you. You'll be a good father."

"I'm going to try my best. That's all anyone can say, right?" He opened the center desk drawer and grabbed a set of keys from the tray. "I'll just get the plans." A moment later, they headed back down the stairs. He held the front door for her then, after unlocking the building next door, ushered her into the dilapidated space.

"Yikes!"

"It looks worse than it is," he said. "There's about fifty years of dust on everything, as best as I can figure out. The last tenant moved out around 1960."

"Before we were born."

"Try to see beyond the dust. Picture tables scattered around. Maybe chandeliers hanging from the ceiling and a fireplace on that wall. We'd polish the hardwood floors, maybe put some rugs under the tables. White tablecloths, those little vases with pastel roses in them." His arm swept the space, painting a picture for her. "And in the back room, a commercial kitchen big enough for an army of pastry chefs to keep up with the demand."

She could see it. She had seen it. His words were her words. She placed one hand on her belly and the other over her mouth to hold in the sob threatening to escape. This was her tea room. The dream she'd only told one person about in all her life—him.

"Hey, hey," he said, hurrying to support her with an arm around her shoulder. "Don't cry."

She dashed tears from her cheeks, but her emotions had stolen her voice.

"I thought you'd be happy."

She nodded. "I am," she cried. "These are…hap-happy tears."

"You like it? You want to see the plans? I wasn't sure what size tables you wanted, so I had the architect draw his rendering with some big ones and some small ones, too." He steered her to a set of sawhorses with an old door on top. He rolled the plans out, anchoring the curled edges with blocks of wood he found on the floor.

Roseanne stared at the top page—the architect's vision for what the inside would look like. He'd captured every detail she had envisioned, weaving them together to create her dream. "It's perfect. Absolutely perfect." God, she'd become a watering pot. She couldn't stop the tears from falling.

"Check out the kitchen. There's room for you to have a test kitchen for all your recipes…so you can do more cookbooks." He flipped the page over to reveal a kitchen fit for a five-star restaurant. "See, this would be your test kitchen over here. It's separate from the tea room kitchen but could be used on special occasions if you needed the extra equipment and space."

"Like for wedding or bridal showers. Or birthday parties."

"Those are great ideas. Ways to maximize the earning potential of the space. You could host things like that during hours you would otherwise be closed. This space was originally a hotel. You could use the guest rooms upstairs as private dining rooms."

"Scott."

"What, sweetheart?"

"This is…"

"For you." He placed his hands on her shoulders and smiled gently down at her.

"This is for you, Roseanne."

"But you could rent this space—"

"Who said I wouldn't be charging you rent?" He chuckled. "I'm a business man, not an idiot."

"Oh."

"But, for my wife, I could maybe discount the rate. You know…for services rendered?" He winked at her, and his grin made it clear what kind of services he had in mind.

"Are you…asking?"

His thumb brushed a tear from her cheek. "This isn't the way I imagined asking, in a dusty old building, but yeah, I am asking." He dropped to one knee and took her hand in his. "Roseanne Meadows, would you please, please marry me?"

Her inability to catch her breath didn't have anything to do with the dust clogging the air. Scott had stolen the air right out of her lungs, just as he had stolen her heart and owned her body. A million things raced through her mind at lightning speed. She'd judged him falsely, assuming things about him that weren't true, while he had seen her for who she was and accepted all of her. She didn't deserve him.

"Roseanne, please," he begged. "All I want is to make you happy. Oh, crap! I almost forgot." He released her hand to dig in his front pants pocket. "I have a ring."

"You do?" If he'd gone to the trouble of getting a ring, then this wasn't some spur of the moment insanity. He'd *planned* on asking her to marry him. Her heart swelled with love for him.

He stood and held a small box out to her. "Open it. Please?"

The small leather-clad box with gold pinstripes around the edges looked old, but she could tell it had been taken care of. She opened the hinged lid and gasped. "Oh, Scott. It's lovely."

"It was my grandmother's engagement ring. She left it to me. I found it when I cleaned out the safe in my apartment."

"You cleaned out your safe?"

"Yeah. The weekend of my parents' anniversary party. Cleaned out the safe, took what I wanted from the place, which wasn't much, and put my apartment up for sale."

"Why?"

"Because it wasn't my home any longer."

She held his gaze, silently questioning.

"My home is wherever you are."

"Scott," she breathed.

He cupped her hand, turning it so he could look at the ring, too. "I didn't think I'd find someone who would want this old thing, but when I looked at it that night, I knew it was meant for you. It's old, nothing like the ones they make today. If you don't like it, I'll buy you anything you want."

"It's perfect." She'd never seen a more beautiful ring. The yellow marquis-cut diamond set in an antique gold filigree band winked at her in the dim light of the old hotel.

"Marry me, Roseanne."

"I shouldn't."

"Why not? What can I do?"

"I shouldn't, but…but I am. If you're

sure."

"I've never been more sure about anything in my life. You're the one, sweetheart. The only one I'll ever want. The only one I'll ever need."

"I want you, too. I need you." It had taken her long enough to admit it, but once she did, a weight lifted off her shoulders.

"Is that a yes? Please tell me it is."

She smiled up at him. "That's a yes, Mr. Ramsey."

"Thank God." Suddenly, he dropped to both knees and pulled her close so he could wrap his arms around her hips. He pressed a soft kiss to her belly. "Did you hear that, buddy? Your mom said she would marry me."

"Scott." She ran her hands through his hair. She'd missed touching him, missed these tender moments they'd always been so good at. He looked up at her. "I love you both. So much."

"We love you, too. So much."

Finally, he rose to frame her face in his hands. He pressed his lips to hers, sealing the deal. "How soon can we get married?”

“How soon do you want to?”

“Yesterday works for me.”

“I’ll see what I can do.” She went up on tiptoes and brushed her lips over his. “I’ve missed you.”

His lips quirked up on the corners. “Why, Ms. Meadows. I do believe you’re propositioning me.”

“I always knew you were smart. So what’s it going to be, mister? Are you going to take me up on the offer?”

“Damn right I am.”

ABOUT THE AUTHOR

USA Today Best-Selling author Roz Lee is the author of over thirty romances. The first, The Lust Boat, was born of an idea acquired while on a Caribbean cruise with her family, and soon blossomed into a five-book series originally published by Red Sage. Following her love of baseball, Roz turned her attention to sexy athletes in tight pants, writing the critically acclaimed Mustangs Baseball series.

Roz has been married to her best friend and high school sweetheart for over four decades. They have two daughters and are the proud grandparents of three adorable grandkids. Roz and her husband live in the wilds of New Jersey with their Labrador Retriever, Bud which is code for Big Unruly Dog.

Even though Roz has lived on both coasts, her heart lies in between, in Texas. A Texan by birth, she can trace her family back to the Republic of Texas. With roots that deep, she says, "You can't ever really leave."

When Roz isn't writing, she's reading or traipsing around the country on one adventure or another. No trip is too small, no tourist trap too cheesy, and no road unworthy of travel.

Visit Roz's Website – www.RozLee.net